READER REVIEWS

"To read *'A Brooklyn Saga..."* is to travel back in time to the real Brooklyn. New Yorkers, you don't know Williamsburg until you've read Angiolillo's and Kule's work! The characters are colorful and nuanced, and details about the neighborhood and the locals who reside in it are so visceral that you can practically taste Caterina's gravy and feel the front steps of her family's stoop under your feet. Angie adds innocence and complexity to the story and provides a compelling and somewhat classic coming-of-age tale set against the gritty city. A joy to read!" —**Alison Caporimo, former deputy editor of *Seventeen* magazine**

"A Brooklyn Saga... is a wonderful and personal representation of how the mixture of characters from many lands came together on the stoops of Brooklyn sidewalks... a revelation of the intricate weavings of our special culture: gritty and fascinating, loving and wonderful. I was profoundly touched by this easy-to-read exposé." — **Dr. James Goldberg, Nominee for the Nobel Prize in Medicine, Santa Fe, New Mexico**

"A Brooklyn Saga... engages like only an evening of gossip with the family can. The characters are... more than enough to give a sense of what life was like during the last century in this little section of the universe called Williamsburg Brooklyn. You'll be richer for meeting these people." — **Darrell Edrich, Client Builders Business Consulting, Clearwater, Florida**

"... Angiolillo's and Kule's superb and clear writing made *A Brooklyn Saga Stories from the Stoop* easy to navigate through all the different names and relationships and geography of Brooklyn, a place I've never visited. I felt like I came to know the characters, all of them. All in all, this is a wonderful story, wonderfully constructed and wonderfully written. So, so enjoyable! Man, oh man!" — **Dwight Noteslinger Mikkelsen, Texas (a.k.a. Foster Kinn,** author of *Freedom's Rush, Tales from The Biker and The Beast*)

* * *

A BROOKLYN SAGA

STORIES FROM THE STOOP

CAROLYN ANGIOLILLO
AND
RONALD JOSEPH KULE

A Brooklyn Saga Stories from the Stoop

by

Carolyn Angiolillo and Ronald Joseph Kule

ISBN: 978-1-7371867-0-0

Library of Congress Cataloging-in-Publication Data
is available on file.

Cover Design: Rebecacovers

Cover Photo: Joe Raskin

Published by CAROLYNBOOKS, L.L.C.

This book may be purchased in bulk at special discounts for sales promotion, corporate gifting, fund-raising, or educational purposes. For information contact cangiolillo@gmail.com.

(Disclaimer: This work is fiction; any similarity to real events, places, or persons is purely coincidental.)

Printed in the United States of America.

DEDICATION

Carolyn Angiolillo:

To my parents,

Louis and Connie Angiolillo

Ronald Joseph Kule:

To Jeremiah and Justin, my son and grandson

To L. Ron Hubbard, a writer's writer."

To my Muse, Yulia Varlakhina.

From Us:

Past, present, and future residents of Williamsburg Brooklyn, may your neighborhood and its legacies live on within your hearts forever.

TABLE OF CONTENTS

INTRODUCTION

In 1802, U.S. Army Chief of Engineers, Colonel Jonathan Williams, surveyed an undeveloped tract of land for a Long Island landowner and real estate investor, Richard M. Woodhull. In his honor, Woodhull named it Williamsburgh.

Williamsburg (as later spelled upon charter in 1852) began as a farmland community. Incorporated into Brooklyn in 1855, its population grew rapidly, eventually housing an integral part of Manhattan's burgeoning workforce that commuted to work and back home by way of the Fulton Ferry across the East River. In 1883, the Brooklyn Bridge spanned the distance, enabling trolley-car and foot traffic. When the Williamsburg Bridge went up in 1903, carriage and rail traffic improved. Five years later, New York City tunneled subway lines under the river a year before the Manhattan Bridge added another overhead crossing.

Williamsburg Brooklyn ("WB") was the first-call melting pot for many newly immigrated

European arrivals. Practically all of WB's earliest residents first passed through Ellis Island, the nation's busiest immigration inspection station. First- and second-generation Italians who left the overcrowded streets and tenements of Manhattan's Lower East Side, dubbed "Little Italy," also moved to WB.

Naturally segregated by a commonly held understanding, a tacit consent, the area's different ethnic groups mainly lived apart. In Greenpoint (a.k.a. "Little Poland") slightly to the north, Polish people were the predominant ethnic group among a mix of German, Irish, and, to a lesser extent, Austrian immigrants. While Black and Puerto Rican immigrants and one of the nation's largest enclaves of Hasidic Jews lived at WB's edges, Italians made up the balance of residents in WB.

From individuals who brought the traditions, customs, and habits of the Old Country sprang the various WB cultures. Italians shared common characteristics, feelings of fellowship, similar attitudes, interests, and goals, and these defined their community. Taste buds, however, ran multi-cultural; people shopped in each other's neighborhoods for palate-pleasing delicacies available from an ever-expanding menu of specialty-food shops based on offerings from different nationalities.

Seasonal changes, passers-by, and other residents' lives added to the eclectic experience of growing up in predominantly Italian WB. When not working, eating, sleeping, shopping, playing indoor card games, or outdoor sports in the parks and on the streets, WB residents cherished one commonly held tradition: sitting outside on the stairs, "stoops," that led up and down to row house and brownstone building front doors. From the stoop, neighbors watched the world pass by, often inviting diverse individuals to stop and connect, if only for an occasional chat. In large part, stoop time defined an individual's outlook on life, living, and death. From the stoop, residents discovered varying degrees of relief from the emotional pressures of day-to-day urban living.

Stoop life offered a smorgasbord of happenings, spaces and times of solace, reminiscences, lively conversations, arguments, impromptu sporting games, and diverse gatherings composed of generations of family, neighbors, friends, even occasional strangers.

The motley atmosphere of one particular WB neighborhood stoop permeates these pages.

What makes for meaningful memories from WB's yesterdays will, we hope, entertain and inspire readers today and well into the future. This historical fiction work focuses on slices of the realities faced by the hard-scrabble individuals who passed through WB, including Carolyn Angiolillo. Any similarity to real WB people, circumstances, events, and incidents is purely coincidental.

CHAPTER 1: WILLIAMSBURG BROOKLYN

Most Italians, Poles, Germans, Irish, and Austrians were of the Catholic faith, giving Catholic parish priests a predominant influence over WB and Greenpoint communities. The priests of The Shrine of the Madonna Church on Havemeyer Street were dynamic, Old Country Italians who dogmatically espoused doctrines of condemnation not easily understood by young children. From their earliest years of tagging along to Sunday Mass with their parents, children in their congregations had difficulty sitting still on the hard pews. Any child's attempt to reconcile an "all-loving Christ" with "Godly punishments" that might rain down upon them and their fellow parishioners, when there were visible contradictions inside of the church walls and outside in the neighborhood, made matters worse.

In this church, the congregation at Mass sat side by side in the pews and made up a gaggle of single persons, small and large families, young couples in love, bitter divorcees, gays, lesbians, mob bosses, acknowledged local prostitutes, and known adulterers. The same mix walked out of Saturday evening confessionals; it sought God's forgiveness by praying hard over the Holy Rosary or reciting the Hail Mary prayer as many times as their priest had recommended from behind closed doors and sliding panels.

The same priests welcomed other known sinners and saints every Sunday morning, including one devout "family," a heterosexual married couple, which regularly brought to church a man who lived openly with them in a *ménage à trois*!

The people of WB understood who was who and what they did publicly or behind closed doors. This uninspected cross-section of humanity tolerated the diversity with mere yawns or an occasional whisper.

After Mass, parishioners filed out of the church. They drifted to their or their relatives' homes to prepare expansive table feasts for traditional, Sunday-afternoon, family get-togethers conducted the way they were back in the Old Country.

For WB youngsters, the stoops outside made Sunday (and everyday) life a lot easier to absorb and far less serious than what, at times, went on inside the house. Inside, the adults ruled the roost and often hit high decibel levels of animated conversation.

Summer days and nights were ice-cream prime-times for kids of all ages passing stoop time chatting, dreaming, or playing games and listening for the distinctive chimes of the ice-cream truck! "Joe the Good Humor Man," dressed in his snappy, white uniform, was the neighborhood hero on hot afternoons and evenings. He delivered Vanilla, Chocolate, and Strawberry Bars that were frozen delights designed by Harry Burt, the first ice-cream bar inventor.

Mr. Softee trucks developed by brothers William and James Conway of Philadelphia offered a competitive choice. Their musical tones captured young people's attention gathered on a certain stoop located on Conselyea Street between Lorimer Street and Union Avenue, the one considered the "most popular gathering spot" of the neighborhood.

Like any other residential community, rough spots and disturbing incidents broke out from time to time in WB's Italian section. Overall, though, the area was a peaceful, hard-working, blue-collar community with a good attitude. In summer, when laborers returned from the local Navy shipyard, local manufacturing facilities, and retail shops, they threw open their apartment windows, releasing the day's accumulated heat and humidity. The sterling sounds of Caruso, Mario Lanza, and other operatic singers filled the air and caressed their neighbors' ears. From this sector and its stoops, life evolved parallel to the nation's confidence, rising to heavenly heights or falling into canyon-deep chasms determined by the cherished winds of American freedoms of choice, economic windfalls, times of duress, and the barometric roller-coastering of world affairs.

This melee of New World whimsy and Italian arias failed to stem the inevitable rising tide of another Old Country holdover, the Mafia. Mob activities brought, at times, murmurs and pleas for mercy or more time from individuals about to get a limb or a kneecap broken, or worse, for not paying a debt or paying late. Although Mob soldiers working at the behest of their capos rarely exercised these extortions in the open, legendary tall tales still traveled the hazardous grapevine of Sunday-dinner-table gossips and stoop-side whisperers.

The WB streets' daily routine maintained an air of safety and congeniality for most people, especially when residents bought goods from retailers within a block or two from home. Local people shopped daily at Joe's Butcher Shop, Tedone's Italian Grocery, Nickie's Fruit Store, Pasquale's Pork Store, Napoli's Bread Shop, and DeLuca's Bakery. Italian individuals and families savored the freshest fruits and meats; among those who did were Luigi and Caterina Carpello and their two daughters, Angelina (Angie) and Jenny (JJ).

When old enough, Angie cradled lists of needed foods written out by her mom, along with the money to buy them, when she visited the retailers alone or with her sister. Her favorite *solo* run was to Tedone's grocery for Italian cold cuts, provolone, and fresh mozzarella. She liked to visit there most when the proprietor was making the fresh cheese. Fascinated, she watched Georgie run hot water into a small sink at the back of the store, cut a piece of curd, soak it in the sink, and, after stretching and pulling it until soft, mold it into braided shapes and bite-size balls. Because Georgie liked Angie stopping by, she often offered her favorite fan freshly made hot mozzarella pieces. Other times, she made prosciutto and provolone sandwiches on Italian bread sprinkled with olive oil, which Angie ate while Georgie cut more cold cuts. When alone, they talked endlessly.

Today after school, Angie had to visit two different stores with her sister.

"Angie, here's the grocery list for the fruits and meats I need today at Nickie's and Joe's Butcher. As usual, I wrapped the money and the lists together. When you get there, give the list and the money to Nickie and the butcher. Remind them to put the change in the bag with the groceries, so you don't lose any of the money."

"Okay, mom. I can do that."

"Good, my dear. And go see if you can tear your sister JJ away from those books she reads all the time, to go with you for company, okay?"

"Yes, mom."

JJ loved to read, but Angie didn't have to beg her to come along this time.

At their eye level in the butcher shop, the two young sisters saw the featured cuts of meat directly in front of them behind the glass display case. The counter was too high for them to see over, but from this vantage point, they watched the butcher go into the cooler room and bring back a whole side of beef, from which he cut the finest, freshest steaks to their mom's order. The girls always brought home the best cuts to be prepared and cooked by Caterina, who was considered one of the best chefs in the neighborhood.

Thus, Angie grew up in the footprints of her family's ancestors and heritage. Being the older sibling, her values and her early childhood experiences year by year molded her personality with the time-honored familial traits of grit, ingenuity, persistence, and plain-old gut instinct.

Luigi, Caterina, Angie, and JJ Carpello came from the "good stock" of different old-country lineages that included the Galliano, Ambrezia, Fiorini, and Carpello families.

CHAPTER 2: FAMIGLIA

Grandfather Domenico Galliano enlisted in the military, fought hard battles, and died far from home in the 1895-96 war between Italy and Ethiopia. He left behind a wife, Rosa, to raise four children, two girls and two boys. Notified of this news, her brother returned to Italy in 1905 and took the two girls to live with him in America. The boys' fates were not so kind: one sold off to another family to make ends meet; the other stayed at home to care for his aging mother.

Bianca Galliano, Rosa's daughter, and her younger sister arrived from Verona at Ellis Island, accompanied by the uncle who oversaw their safe passage. He took them to live at his place on Mulberry Street in Manhattan's Little Italy, where he and his wife cared for and protected them until they grew to adulthood.

Once old enough, Bianca took work in a garment factory on the Lower East Side. She fell in love with a tailor employed there, Pietro Carpello, a native of San Giorgio Lucano, Italy, in

Basilicata. They married in 1919, bought a two-story, two-family house in Borough Park Brooklyn, and started a family that eventually included two sons, Luigi and Donato.

Pietro rented out the upstairs to another couple, Carlo and Isabella Dalligio, opening the door to something like a page torn from a Shakespearean tragedy.

Though madly in love with his wife, Pietro worked long hours at the shop. He didn't mind the work, and he advanced rapidly to a management position within the company. Unfortunately, his new, heavier workload left Bianca to manage the household alone and raise their two growing boys.

Despite several years happily married and while still in love with her husband, Bianca came to feel increasingly lonely and abandoned. She missed his company.

Coincidentally, on the days that Isabella worked, Carlo had his days off from his job, leading to Bianca and him spending time together. Carlo, Bianca, Luigi, and Donato soon frequented the sandy beach on nearby Coney

Island. Rankled by this, growing suspicious, and feeling distant from his wife, Pietro hired a private investigator to follow them. Eventually, he discovered through photo evidence a torrid affair going on behind his back! Incensed, he filed for a divorce and custody of his boys.

In those days, especially in New York State, any woman unfaithful to her husband was overtly shunned and labeled an adulteress. Bianca lost the custody battle and was permitted only once-a-month visitation rights with her sons—at that, under supervision. The ruling forced the uncle who brought her to America, who now lived in WB, back into her life.

At the time of the divorce proceedings, Bianca was pregnant! Unsure of the unborn's parentage, Pietro fought to have the expected newborn's last name *not* be his, but the court ruled otherwise, stating that Bianca had conceived while still legally married to him. Upon the birth of the infant, Bianca, alone, named her Margarita Carpello.

Economic depression claimed the early Thirties, and Pietro did not escape the downturn unscathed. After working at one garment factory for many years, he lost his position there. Forced out of town to find similar work, he moved south to North Carolina, enrolled his two boys in a Catholic elementary school, and took a new wife, Maria, with whom he had a son named Antonio.

In 1936, Pietro returned to New York and worked for Solomon Brothers & Company in the Gretsch Building on Broadway in WB. He and his family lived in the Bronx—another Little Italy—to be closer to his parents, brothers, and sisters. Subway train commutes from home to work and back made the new arrangement easy.

* * *

At age 12, Giuseppe Ambrezia and his older brother came to New York City from Naples, Italy, by lowest-cost steerage class on the ship's bottom deck. In 1920, he married Gabriella Fiorini and opened a café in a rented storefront in the building where they lived on Union Avenue. He served espresso and pastries to patrons stopping by to chat over a cup of coffee, those playing pool, and others playing the "Italian Lottery" (aka, "betting the numbers"). In a couple of years, the Ambrezias had a daughter, Caterina, later followed by Rosa Maria.

A proud father, Giuseppe explained his extra-curricular side business to friends and associates, "The café puts only a few crumbs on my table; taking numbers helps me feed my family. I'm just trying to make ends meet"—a refrain echoed inside many Italian apartments.

Having kept the antés small, Giuseppe believed that his wife and daughters never knew what he did to bring home, from time to time, additional provisions for the family dining table. However, the night local authorities received an anonymous tip about his affairs and showed up at his apartment door without warning, he discovered otherwise!

The local police thought they had caught Giuseppe red-handed with his hands deep into the illegal gambling cookie jar. Unannounced and at a late hour, they came without a warrant. A quick-thinking-and-acting young Caterina, moving rapidly under the astonished stares of her younger sister, snatched up all the scribbled sheets of names and numbers. She had seen these in her father's work area, and now she stuffed them into a clothespin bag, reeling them far out on the laundry line outside the kitchen window. The investigating officers' intense search throughout the whole apartment never found one scrap of incriminating evidence!

Relief and tears overcame Giuseppe despite his disbelief that his ten-year-old was so aware of his side business when his daughter told him where she had hidden the number sheets.

In the Ambrezia apartment, the police incident, merely one of a long chain of challenging events the family would face together, added to Caterina's broad education in the volatile ways of street life in WB. As a smaller child, she had already witnessed someone killed by Tommy gunfire while the victim attempted a call in a phone booth!

Unlike in other neighboring households, Giuseppe took care of his numbers business by himself. In other homes, wives took chances alongside their husbands to help them manage their affairs. They recruited their children to deliver slips of betted numbers and cash wrapped inside newsprint pages to bookies on the street corner so casually that an outsider would be hard-pressed to discern anything illegal going on, let alone in broad daylight!

In the year of their third daughter Sofia's birth, the City of New York ordered Giuseppe to vacate his café because it was in the proposed Brooklyn-Queens Expressway path. All occupants on that parcel of land, including the neighborhood Catholic church, had to relocate. On a brighter note, the city provided the families, churches, priests, and nuns with enough funds to help them find other places to live. The church purchased a parcel of land a few blocks away on Havemeyer Street and built a new church building. The Ambrezia family located another apartment and storefront suitable for a cafe on Metropolitan Avenue around the corner from where they had lived. Inexplicably, though, the relocated nuns from the same church ended up right next to the café, bringing on complaints from them about the activities of the men who frequented the café to "... play pool, have one or two espressos, and whatever else they do in there."

The church forced a shutdown of the cafe. Gabriella and Giuseppe, rightfully upset, pleaded with church representatives to help them, explaining they had barely enough money to feed the family, which now included the new infant. Heartlessly, church administration officials ignored their pleas and abandoned the Ambrezias, leaving the family less to eat, sometimes only a few potatoes and a piece of hard bread for dinner.

When Giuseppe finally located another place suitable for his café, their lives soon settled back to normal, perhaps in part because of his big-hearted personality. Standing short of stature at five-foot-six and obesely heavy, he was street smart, despite not knowing how to read or write. Due to his educational deficiency, he devised an ingeniously simple system for keeping his accounts straight without too many written records. It consisted of made-up, fake names based on the various physical appearances of his customers, like "Shorty with

Fat Nose," "Curly Head," "Limpo," and "Three Fingers," among others. If the police ever captured one of his lists, they might first check race cards at the local horse tracks only to find zero equine entries with such names and have to let go for lack of evidence, once again, one of their prime suspects!

Giuseppe understood that to get by, people would do whatever they felt they must to survive, no matter how distasteful, even borrow money. In the Forties, using the cash generated by his numbers operation, he generously offered small loans to locals he knew were in need, conducting this business from the backroom of his cafe. Though "loan sharking," Giuseppe didn't charge high rates of interest or break legs or kneecaps if someone ran a bit late with a payment. He worked *with* his customers because he enjoyed helping people he knew.

His local competitor, the Mafia, mostly targeted much larger fish. They looked the other way when it came to Giuseppe's side operation. His loan dealings were too small for them to care about; also, they understood that his only purpose was to feed and clothe his family—his typical loans were strictly five-and-dime, a variety of five-to-ten-dollar totals. While today, those would be small beans, such meager amounts then helped people feed whole families. For that reason, and because Mob personnel enjoyed Giuseppe's fun personality while considering him penny-ante and not a serious competitor, Mafia bosses not only let him stay in business but also alive as long as God might wish. His other saving grace was that the made-men whom Giuseppe met and befriended came away with the impression that he was an "Even-Steven kind of guy" and an "All-Right Joe." So Mafia capos left him alone.

* * *

When America joined the Allied effort in WW II, Luigi and Donato Carpello, now young men, enlisted in the army and fought in Europe. Luckily, they returned intact and able to work with their father, learn his trade, and become established tailors, which, of course, made Pietro proud.

One day, however, Donato openly expressed a serious disagreement with his stepmother. Hearing of this situation and thinking his son disrespectful despite his apology to Maria, Pietro disowned him, saying, "I don't care to bother with you anymore." His decision also caused an estrangement between the two blood brothers, an open wound that festered for years.

During the war, Donato and Luigi had lost contact with their mom Bianca. Despite several letters both her sons had sent her, she never replied. Now that Donato stood separated from his father and brother—heartbroken and no longer working at the shop, he took a position as a train conductor and reached out to her. At first, happy to reconnect, he realized he still had feelings of loss and abandonment associated with her; consequently, he only saw her on holidays.

Meanwhile, before his sons returned from the war in Europe, Pietro kept an eye on one of his most favored employees, Caterina Ambrezia, whom he liked as a possible spouse for Luigi. He openly promoted this liaison to her in his trademark broken English,

"Caterina, my darling, I havva nice-a son, Luigi. When-a he comes outta da army, I'm-a gonna make you meet him. I wanna you be my daughter-in-law!"

The trouble was, upon his return from military duty, Luigi developed an eye for another woman, Nina, whom he dated regularly. There seemed something long-term at first, but the relationship fizzled, and Nina and Luigi broke up. Seeing this, when alone with his son in Caterina's presence, Pietro introduced Luigi to her, as promised, and stood back to watch the sparks fly.

At first, they were no match made in Heaven. Caterina observed that Luigi always wore finely tailored suits and thought that he must be a snob. Yet, not long after, approached by him for a coffee date, she accepted. Once they knew each other better, they began serious dating and were prime candidates for a couple of Cupid's marriage arrows before long.

Meeting her family, Luigi fell in love with Caterina's parents, who, believe it or not, lived in WB right around the corner from Luigi's great-uncle's place—where he visited his mother! With the Ambrezias, he found the kind of family life he had dreamed of someday having: jovial parents with a warm home that welcomed all types of people to visit anytime—an atmosphere her parents created out of necessity and time-honored cultural habits.

Beyond friendships, the Ambrezias' toughness also showed. In WB neighborhoods, people relied upon one another and did whatever had to be done to get by, legal or quasi-legal. Caterina's parents, who survived the Spanish Flu, the Great Depression, and two World Wars, made ends meet by performing contract sewing work, running a billiard café, cleaning schools, and owning and running a dry-goods store. Of course, Giuseppe ran his numbers and loan sharked—whatever helped his family ride over obstacles that came their way, which defined to Luigi what this family was about and how different they were from his own.

Luigi's accepted marriage proposal to Caterina in 1949 thrilled the Ambrezia and

Carpello family members. In subsequent years, the Carpellos and Ambrezias got on like one giant family. They entertained each other regularly on Sundays. After dinner, Pietro often performed on the mandolin as most of the others danced along. Mingled within this wider circle, extended family members came to know each other well, delighted to attend two weddings in subsequent years when both Sofia and Antonio married their high-school sweethearts, Robert and Anita, respectively.

The families vacationed for a couple of weeks every summer in Monticello, New York. When they returned, Giuseppe hosted large barbecue parties in his backyard, often inviting both families, their relatives, and relatives of relatives. These cheerful gatherings of adults and children marked by dancing, singing, dining al fresco on steaks, burgers, frankfurters, Italian potato salad, broccoli rabe, and corn on the cob consumed in large quantities, as well as, of course, nuts, fruits, pastries, and plenty of espressos satisfied many palates!

To celebrate their 40th wedding anniversary, Giuseppe announced he wanted to show his bride his homeland. Born in America, she never saw Italy and was apprehensive about taking such a long trip. After many discussions, they finally decided to go and publicly announced their plan.

The large extended family gathered on the pier with invited friends and boarded the recently built SS Michelangelo. Following their grand tour of the vessel, their Bon-Voyage party became a gay celebration bubbling with champagne, myriad food choices, and colorful balloons. When the time arrived for good-byes to everyone, including their grandchildren, Angie, JJ, Sofia, and Robert's children, Daniella and Christopher, they all hugged profusely. The entourage returned to the pier dock and waved, staying as long as possible to watch the magnificent cruise liner slip its moorings and steam out of New York Harbor, bound for Italy.

Angie's grandparents wrote home often, sending letters and postcards from the various places they visited. They reported that they were having a great time meeting with relatives, making new friends, and feasting on lots and lots of fresh foods daily.

Suddenly, misfortune arrived the day they both got stomach viruses. After a couple of weeks, Giuseppe felt better, but Gabriella's condition declined. Her health condition required a return cruise home earlier than planned.

Upon the elderly couple's return, Aunt Rosa Maria, Angie's parents, and Angie met the weary travelers at the Manhattan pier. Right away, they noticed that Gabriella was not at all well. Days later, Beth Israel Hospital diagnosed her with Typhoid Fever. The diagnosis forced the whole family to undergo once-a-week vaccination shots delivered over several weeks at the Board of Health on Bushwick Avenue, further confusing the grandchildren, especially Angie, who had not previously experienced anything so tragic. Making matters worse, the hospital permitted only adults to visit Gabriella in quarantine, a severe blow to Angie's fragile emotions!

Caterina, observing her daughter's sadness, one day brought her to Stuyvesant Park. Sitting on a bench facing the hospital, she pointed to the room occupied by her mother.

Looking at her grandmother's room from the park bench was strong consolation for Angie. Glad that her beloved grandmother was not so far away, she could almost feel her presence.

Grandmother Gabriella did come home from the hospital. She brought with her little "Lassie" plush-toy dogs for Angie and JJ, knowing how much her granddaughters loved the television show on Sunday nights and how many times she had watched them kiss the TV screen whenever Lassie sat and put up her paw. But that was the last time in which Angie saw her grandmother. After only a few days, the older woman returned to the hospital. Two weeks later, she died.

Told that her grandmother went to Heaven, Angie could not grasp what happened to her precious relative, who always felt more like a mother than a grandparent to her, or why she was no longer around to make breakfast for her in the morning.

The loss of their most beloved relative devastated the entire family. Giuseppe blamed himself for taking her on the trip to Italy, although family and friends stopped by to reassure him that he had not caused her demise.

The family atmosphere never was the same without their matriarch's presence; its conscience had died with her.

Her grandmother's death so numbed Angie's heart center that only playing with her plush toy Lassie brought her solace.

CHAPTER 3: A TYPICAL DAY

Angie's feelings eventually healed with time, parental support, new friends in school, running more errands, and outings with her sister and mom.

Once Caterina started taking her girls to shop at Natan Borlam in Brooklyn's Jewish neighborhood, the regular trips became a cherished mother/daughter tradition. They walked down Havemeyer Street, stopped to buy pickles from the deli's barrel, and shared corned beef or pastrami on rye bread sandwiches at Pastrami King down the block from Natan's. On other days, they shopped in Greenpoint at Peter Pan's Bakery for the finest donuts made by the Poles or visited the local German delicatessen for a Chocolate Blackout Cake.

Today, as Catarina wrote out another food list at home, Angie and JJ munched on a snack she prepared earlier for them: cauliflower pancakes made from chopped cauliflower sprinkled with pepper, mixed into a savory batter, and fried.

"Girls, tonight I'm making macaroni with meatballs in the gravy. Angie, go to Joe's Butcher Shop and get two pounds of chopped meat."

Happy to hear that her mom was making one of her and JJ's favorites, Angie answered, "Okay, off I go!"

Caterina prepped and assembled the ingredients upon Angie's return, a mix of chopped beef, eggs, breadcrumbs, milk—not water, and a generous gathering of fresh minced garlic sprinkled with parsley and cooked, of course, only in olive oil. The redolent smell of the heated olive oil and garlic permeated the house, and the aroma wafted out the open windows and throughout the entire block, if not all, of the adjacent streets!

Watching her mom, Angie asked, "Mom, what else do you need? I'm ready. Let me help you."

Caterina, constantly moving among her foodstuffs, directed both of her girls: "Angie, get me two cans of tomato sauce in the closet so I can start the gravy. JJ, go by Anna's across the street and ask her for some breadcrumbs. I only need a little, and I don't want to send you or your sister back to the store."

"Sure, Mom!" said JJ, who knew that asking would not be an imposition because there had been times when Anna came to them, begging for some sugar because she had run out.

"Hello, JJ! What a surprise! Nice to see you!"

"Anna, Mom says she needs breadcrumbs for her meatballs."

"No problem, I have some extra for her." Anna went inside and came back with two cups of breadcrumbs.

WB people were like that, people knew people, and they helped each other, even those from different backgrounds. One Yugoslavian family on the block had many children to feed and not a lot of income to make ends meet. Block neighbors regularly chipped in and cooked a little extra, sending food plates over to the "Yugo's" (an affectionate name they liked).

They aren't Italian, but they're part of our block, so we help them was the thought.

Back home, Caterina thanked her daughter and mixed the breadcrumbs into the chopped meat, which she then molded and cooked while Angie and JJ completed their homework at the kitchen table.

A bit later, she said, "Thank you, girls. Here are a couple of meatballs to eat."

After they finished, Caterina asked them to set the table for dinner.

"Make sure there are plates for my sister Rosa Maria and my father. I expect them to join us for dinner this evening."

Meanwhile, Caterina cracked more eggs into a new bowl of mixed ingredients and kneaded them into more meatballs. As she often did, she thought about "Mike, the Egg Man," whom she knew for many years, who turned out to be quite an entrepreneur out of necessity.

Mike lost his storefront shop because of the impending expressway coming through his location, but, unwilling to give up, he took his business directly to the streets of WB. He fashioned a pushcart from a flat 6' x 6' board mounted on wagon wheels and then sold directly to his customers a selection of different egg sizes and various fruits and vegetables. Pushing the cart through the streets, he called out in broken English,

"Mike'a, da hegga man
here! Mike'a da hegga man
here!"

Once he stopped in the middle of a block, everyone came out and supported his WB shop-on-wheels as Mike pitched hard,

"Have'a taste-a, see if you
like-a. You like-a, you buy."

I liked buying his eggs and fruits, Caterina mused, a broad smile spreading across her face. *I really miss him.*

A typical Italian cook, she always prepared more food than immediately needed, thinking *You never know who will stop by!*

When, as if on cue, one of her regular visitors, Tony, a family friend who performed handyman jobs around the Carpello house, stopped by to say hello, she greeted him profusely, "Tony, welcome! Come sit down," clearing an open space for him at the kitchen table.

He replied, “I smell meatballs cooking! How ‘bout some of them on Italian bread with a little gravy?”

“Take a seat at the table. I just made some fresh.” And then she served him “a nice meatball sandwich” with a cold Coca-Cola.

As soon as Tony left the house, Caterina’s first cousin, Anna, rang the bell.

“Hello, Anna, so nice to see you.”

“So nice to see you, too. Here, I brought you some fresh tomatoes from my garden.”

“*Grazie*, I’m glad you stopped by. Have dinner with us. It will be ready in about an hour. Also, Rosa Maria and my husband will be home from work soon, and my father should be walking through the door at any minute. They’ll both be joining us. Sit down. Have a meatball. I just made them.”

“Thank you, Caterina.”

“Buona Giornata,” said Luigi upon returning home from his new position as a sanitation worker. As he took a seat on the living room couch, the doorbell rang.

"JJ, go answer the door," said Caterina.

"Who is it... 'The Fixture'?" asked Luigi. (Angie's friend, Francesca Panarelli, visited their home so many times he nicknamed her.)

"No, it's your cousin Tessie," announced JJ.

Caterina, wiping her hands on a dishcloth, walked out of the kitchen and greeted her.

"Come in, Tessie. Stay for dinner. You can tell us all about your trip to Italy."

"Oh, what a trip! We all had such a great time. Italy was fabulous!"

As the family ate, Tessie regaled everyone about her recent travels with her fellow parishioners and Father Cuccarelli, the Catholic parish priest whose Masses they all attended. She capped her presentation with a gem: "You'll never guess what happened on the trip! Father Cuccarelli introduced all of us to *his mistress and illegitimate son* when we visited Napoli! Can you believe they live in a villa there?!"

Cousin Anna blessed herself with the sign of the cross. Giuseppe retorted, “I’m not surprised. Priests’ souls are blacker than the robes they wear!”

The level of excitement over the details rose with the volume of their voices as they discussed the pros and cons of the unusual pairing they had just heard about from Tessie. Rosa Maria suggested that maybe Father Cuccarelli was a late-comer to his calling and that he might have had a relationship with the boy’s mother before he became a priest, explaining why he did not hide the connection!

Giuseppe snapped, “Nonsense! This kind of living is normal in Italy.”

Everyone at the table knew that probably he was right, and his remark gave them something else to consider. Finally, the conversation simmered down, followed by a few choice words, a little disagreement, and some nervous laughter.

Toasting with a glass of wine, *“Buona Salute!”* Giuseppe moved the tabletop discussion to other “news of the day,” but not before Angie had taken it all in, as children often will. At her age, left alone to make some sense of what she heard, she could not comprehend the story's full import. The words and other impressions impacted her and shaped her personality as much as puberty would eventually sculpt her pre-teen body. She got up and walked outside.

Later, as the sun fell across the row house rooftops and the last of the relatives left the Carpello house, Angie and JJ sat out on the stoop and waited for some friends to stop by, happy to breathe some fresh air.

Hearing a familiar bell-tone ring, Caterina came outside, pressed some money into Angie's palm, and pointed down the block. Turning her head, Angie saw the "Pie-Truck Man" approaching. Gleefully, she nudged JJ, who, as usual, was buried in a book. Both girls jumped up, ran to the street pavement, and, with big grins on their faces, eagerly waited for the driver to park his truck in an open space.

The happily married couple sold truckloads of fresh pies they home-baked from scratch with fresh ingredients. While one parked the truck, the other walked up and down the sidewalk, ringing a hand-held bell and announcing their arrival with a simple refrain, "'Pie Man here!"

The Carpello sisters knew what to buy because just about every week, they selected a pie from the offered choices of fresh Apple, Blueberry, or Coconut Custard. The last being Caterina's favorite, they eagerly chose that one now and returned to the stoop to eat slices of pie with her.

CHAPTER 4: THE BOUGH BREAKS

Angie enjoyed this stage of her life in no small part because of the love and happiness generated by her parents, the Italian WB atmosphere, and the overall way members of her larger family of families' got along with each other.

Unfortunately, an unexpected, devastating event would soon shock the whole family! Speaking to a few of his friends, Giuseppe leaned on the railing next to the stoop leading down to the Italian Social Club he frequented. The rusty metal suddenly gave way, propelling his body three feet down and through one of the two glass-pane windows beside the entrance door. He suffered numerous lacerations to his head.

After the ambulance team rushed the 76-year-old to St. Catherine's Hospital and ER doctors finished his initial treatment round, nurses under doctors' orders permitted only adult family members and friends to visit him, again saddening Angie. The sudden initial shock of the accident combined with this restriction left her shaken up, scared, and lonely, which went unnoticed by others because of how the trauma affected the whole family.

Giuseppe eventually returned home, and Angie was happy to see him again. But he was not well. Hardly able to talk, within a few weeks, he died.

Desperation slammed into Angie, who shuddered to think who might be next to die in her family. A devastating fear in her heart prevented her from easily navigating this loss of her beloved grandpa so soon after losing her grandma.

Friends and extended family, too, were demoralized. Two family tragedies in as many years made the healing harder and recovery longer.

More upset was to come. A few months later, the larger family's spotlight narrowed and focused on a nearly invisible crack in their love and respect for each other, which threatened to blow their entire family-friendly world apart. Luigi noticed that his younger half-brother

Antonio wore silk suits and socks and thought this odd because Antonio worked as a tailor with their father, and their shop did not manufacture silk menswear. He suspected that his half-brother's leisure-time activities likely also involved dealing with illegal substances. To his surprise, Antonio rebuffed Luigi when he broached the subject to him.

" 'Va fongool, Luigi!' Mind your own business. You don't know what you are talking about!"

This vociferous reply fired up Luigi's greater concern that his half-brother might be up to no good. He told his father his suspicions and what happened between the two brothers.

Unexpectedly, Pietro took sides, choosing Antonio's story over Luigi's. He told Luigi that he was crazy to suspect something like that of his half-brother.

The close-knit fabric of the family weakened and wore thin. Emotionally tattered at its edges, the family's door opened to the possibility of more discordant drafts of frigid air.

Sure enough, an unfortunate incident showed up and shattered the fragile family unit.

Pietro's wife, Maria, lay in St. Barnabas, hospitalized with an unexpected illness, and no one notified Luigi. When he discovered her stay too late to call her there, he called his father, asking why no one informed him. Pietro angrily rebuked his son again, this time for not visiting his stepmother. On several phone calls, Luigi tried to explain that he never knew that Maria lay in the hospital, but his ardent pleas for understanding and forgiveness caught no wind. Even after several of his son's visits to his home, pleading for compassion and forgiveness, Pietro would not give in and forgive Luigi.

Upset and frustrated, Luigi confided the situation to someone he looked up to like a second father, Dominic Chichi, co-owner with his brothers of family-owned Chichi's Bar and Restaurant. Dominic knew the Ambrezia family well, having entertained them many times in their bar-only days. After Luigi married Caterina and the couple moved in only a few doors away from the restaurant, the family dined there more frequently. And after his girls were born,

Luigi tended bar there part-time to bring a little more money into his household. For years, every night after dinner at home, Luigi visited Chichi's and placed a bet on a number. On Friday nights, whenever Pietro came for dinner at his son's house, he and Luigi went to Chichi's for drinks and to talk with Dominic, whose company Pietro enjoyed.

Luigi also met with his admired and trusted parish priest, Father Vaccaro, outside of the confessional booth.

Both men agreed to intercede on Luigi's behalf, but Pietro would not listen to their supplications.

Caterina, incensed by her father-in-law's stubbornness and having known him longer than she knew her husband, called to inquire what was going through his mind. Pietro ignored her pleas on her husband's behalf, repeating over and over, "I do not want to lose another wife."

Luigi called again, and this time his father completely rebuffed him.

"Don't call me anymore. I don't want to lose another wife. You live your life, and I will live mine," adding with mob-like bravado, despite others besieging him not to, "I will cut off my right arm before I change my mind!"

And, just like that, Angie and JJ never again saw their grandparents, Uncle Antonio or Aunt Anita.

After that, plenty of tears spilled on the stoop for a long time.

Although Angie's grandfather had disowned them, Luigi and his full-brother Donato welcomed a renewed connection on a brighter note. He also told his daughters about the brother he had, whom they had never heard about or met. Angie and JJ learned that Donato was married and that he and his wife, Gianna, had three children, Donato Jr., who was 18, Andrea, 14, and Michael, eight years old. The girls also learned that Grandmother Maria was their grandfather's *second* wife, meaning they had another grandmother, Bianca, their father's and uncle's mother. They also had an Aunt Margarita, their father's and uncle's sister, who had four children with her husband, Uncle Vinnie!

Caterina welcomed her husband's reconciliation with his brother, and she loved that their daughters knew, at last, the truth about his family!

Angie, surprised, let her mind assess the situation in light of the new information and then confided to her sister almost in disbelief:

I miss seeing grandpa,
Uncle Antonio, and Aunt Anita,
but I don't miss my step-
grandma Maria; I never liked
her, anyway. She wasn't warm
and tender like Grandma
Gabriella, and she didn't smile
that often.

The family's split left Angie disheartened, especially when she looked at her father and saw a sadness in his eyes. Still, the family held bright spots for her and JJ when Luigi and Donato spent time getting reacquainted and talking about Bianca. Luigi had not seen his mother since he entered the military, and he asked his brother if he had been in touch with her. Donato, surmising that Bianca only wanted her daughter Margarita in her life, replied that they had an off-again, on-again relationship fraught with arguments. At this point, he and their mother talked only on Christmas Day by phone.

Eventually, several weeks later, Uncle Donato and Aunt Gianna invited his brother's family to their home in Carroll Gardens, Brooklyn, seven miles away from Williamsburg, a quick drive by car.

Angie and JJ happily met their new uncle, aunt, and cousins that day. After that, they saw each other regularly. Angie particularly enjoyed visiting her extended family on Sunday evenings. That was when her uncle made homemade pizzas—"... the best-ever I ever ate..."—made with homemade pizza dough, fresh tomato sauce, fresh mozzarella, and Parmigiano-Reggiano cheese.

In turn, cousins Donato, Andrea, and Michael loved to visit Angie's house because they knew that Aunt Caterina's fresh macaroni and gravy with sausage, famous meatballs, and braciole would be on the table. But the best part was sitting out on the stoop with Angie and JJ among their many friends who stopped by from time to time to chat, play street games, or tell stories and listen to gossip.

Unfortunately, stoop gossip carried news far and wide, not all of it good. A day arrived that brought terrible information about Antonio. Earlier word had it that he fell into the short end of a run of drug trades and owed a lot of money to the wrong people. The adults knew Pietro had bailed out Antonio many times and that his son's unsavory behavior never changed. Over time, details coming in had been sketchy at best until, heartbreakingly, while reading *The Daily News* on the stoop, Luigi learned that a man shot in the South Bronx at close range five times in his back was his half-brother. As reported, after hearing gunshots, neighbors witnessed a man gasping for air and whispering for help. Though someone called 911, Antonio died on the street.

The unfortunate turn of events dismayed everyone who knew and loved him, especially Luigi, who, bitter, thought his father never tried to open his eyes to the truth about Antonio's life and habits, failing to save him.

This event and others experienced by Angie while growing up in her Italian neighborhood helped her mature, defined her basic purpose, and determined how she might want to express herself as an adult.

In no small way, the pressures of Angie's life aided her development of adept agility at handling whatever life presented to her. An important trait because—she never knew this was coming—one day, she would meet a Chinese man who would walk down her block to her stoop, learn more about her over time, and propel her living kaleidoscope to a place she could never imagine on her own.

To survive this path laid out by Fate, Angie would need to call on every bit of the WB blood, culture, and traditions that coursed through her authentic Italian DNA. Coming trials of adversity would set her and the Chinese man on time tracks that would lead them to an inevitable and harrowing collision, which, at this moment, neither could see coming!

CHAPTER 5: WENGCHAN LIANG

Wengchan Liang grew up in the farmlands of southern China. Born in 1935, he lived a rural, peaceful existence until the Chinese civil war entered his village and radically altered China's course and his outlook on life. After communist insurgents forced him to witness the senseless slaughter of his innocent, agrarian parents in 1945, the Kuomintang National Revolutionary Army (KMT) rescued, recruited, and trained him in weapons of war and hand-to-hand combat to help them stand against the surging communists. Broken emotionally, he was ripe for his involuntary escort to the training center, and there he discovered he could vent his grief and anger. However, his chances for long-term survival dropped immeasurably when the communists defeated the KMT in 1949. His army's loss and the installment of the PRC's (Peoples' Republic of China) new governance under communist rule made Wengchan's potential to survive past more than a few months look slim. Numbed by what he had seen and done, he almost didn't care if he lived or died. The bloodshed he witnessed and the atrocities he committed under orders had taken a severe emotional toll on him. He was almost gone, despite his young age.

Suddenly, through a stroke of luck, a reed of a chance to exit China in the dead of night aboard a freight ship that would slip away without navigation lights opened to him.

His daring dash for salvation, unfortunately, came with a heavy price: a duel to the death, a saber fight, against another youthful refugee for the last open position on the vessel, which almost cost Wengchan an eye and did attach a permanent scar to his right cheek, which, later, he would cover with makeup.

His opponent fared less well.

Victorious, Wengchan humbly boarded the ship while his body still breathed precious warm air and life. But his soul was barely alive, for the deliberate act of killing one more man surfaced in him a ruthless, cold-blooded outlook that would propel him toward a lonely, solitary existence devoid of many pleasures.

The heavily laden freighter bound for Naples, Italy, steamed westward through the Indian Ocean, Red Sea, Suez Canal, Mediterranean Ocean, and the Tyrrhenian Sea.

Passage onboard the rusty vessel was not a free ride for anyone on board. Wengchan worked in food preparation among other men, ersatz galley workers from different nationalities. Gradually, he established camaraderie with a cross-section of the lively crew, though, at first, he kept mostly to himself, being a fish out of water. Bit by bit, hearing several different languages slung back and forth, he picked up a smattering of usable phrases that he understood, including English, which drew him out of his shell.

Wengchan struck up an acquaintance with another man from China, Zhou-lin, who performed as the galley's dishwasher. On short breaks, they chanced to learn more about each other's past. The other man revealed that he had originally intended to go to New Zealand with several other extended family members also interested in living far away from the homeland oppression. His group planned to work among other Chinese immigrants in the gold mines of the island nation. Like Wengchan's experience, albeit on the losing end of the bargain, Zhou-lin gave up to one of his female cousins the last position available on the vessel headed to Auckland, sacrificing his opportunity and offering her a chance for a better life as a Kiwi. That choice forced his passage on the ship on which he and Wengchan stood.

Despite constant, vivid memories of his parents' demise and other horrific scenes from the civil war playing in his mind, Wengchan gradually accepted the soothing salve of the ocean air, the constant motions of the sea-worthy freighter plowing through warm waters, and the continual hum of the ship's engines. Familiar vibrations not only lulled him to sleep at night but also woke him up to new hopes on more than a score of morning twilights.

The trip consumed 35 days—enough time for his emotions to lighten and to permit his determination of what kind of work he might want to do to survive on dry land. Once the beautiful coastline of Italy came into view on the horizon, Wengchan knew he would have to quickly find a safe place to sleep and a solid job for income. Fortunately, immediately upon disembarking, he landed work loading and unloading cargo at the docks.

The next ten backbreaking years of his life turned out good for his morale, sheer exhaustion often thrusting to the back of his mind his nightmarish memories of the horrors that he would never forget. The best he could do was stabilize and find a balance between his past, present, and future. Eventually, with a new awareness of future possibilities, he developed a less-than-bitter attitude. And then good fortune unexpectedly rained upon him!

Taking a day off from the docks, Wengchan visited Nola, a district of Naples in the south of Italy. After sightseeing all morning, he hired a taxi to return him to the docks in the mid-afternoon. Blue-sky sunlight accented the rich colors of fully grown, leafy olive trees lining the edges of the road. The carefree day filled with sunlight belied looming darkness about to change its mood.

Halfway to his destination, on a narrow, rural, switchback roadway, Wengchan found himself in the crosshairs of a planned shootout between two opposing Mafia families, one of which intended to take out the other's caporegime!

A small band of local mafiosos positioned themselves at one of the hairpin curves halfway down the hillside, ready to assassinate their target. The staged accident scene set in place and designed to bring traffic to a halt on approach to the tight turn gave the marauding gang a surprise element. They hoped this multi-second advantage ahead of their target's possible escape would guarantee their mission's success. They would first disable the capo's bodyguard soldiers with rapid, first-strike gunfire and then take out their prey.

Toting automatic weapons, the capo's armed guards stood on all of the vehicles' sideboards, including the one in which the capo sat in the backseat.

Unaware of the pending danger, Capo Lorenzo Abatelli busied himself reading as best he could the local newspaper while the procession inched along.

And then all hell broke loose!

The advance vehicle's driver spotted the staged "accident" from only a few yards away. He slammed on his brakes, causing a chain reaction that involved three other trailing vehicles.

Abatelli's body jutted forward. In an attempt to arrest his tumble, he grabbed the side door handle, pushing the door open and throwing the unfortunate soldier on the sideboard of his car onto the steep, rough roadside terrain. A hail of bullets from a sniper hidden in the branches of an olive tree instantly riddled the soldier. The slurry of shots signaled a cross-fire startup against the other guards from strategically placed enemies on both sides of the road.

Seeking cover, Abatelli threw himself from his vehicle onto the dirt roadway, hurting his right leg so severely that he could not roll or crawl his way under his car where he might survive the skirmish. He would be a sitting duck once the unseen opposition took out his defensive forces!

From the back seat of his taxi—the last vehicle of the stopped cars, Wengchan watched the event quickly evolve and unfold in front of him. Seeing the older man on the roadway in obvious pain and unable to protect himself, he leaped from his vehicle. Turning toward the sniper's location, he aimed and threw one of the knives that he kept under the folds of his tunic-style shirt, slicing the sniper's jugular and killing him instantly.

Next, a fast-moving gunman running with a cocked pistol in his hand attempted to get close for a sure-kill shot at the capo's head. However, blinded by his mission, he failed to see his Chinese adversary hurtling toward his ankles. Wengchan swiveled his torso and legs around the assassin, instantly dropping him. With a second swift move, he repositioned his legs around the gangster's neck, squeezed hard, and twisted the assailant's life out of him.

Abatelli's remaining soldiers eliminated the rest of the infamous crew of would-be assassins. Astonished by Wengchan's speed and unusual killing method, they recognized that he saved their capo's life and surrounded him for his safety.

Abatelli, of course, was beyond grateful to Wengchan and wanted to show his gratitude to the young man. He ordered a soldier to ride in the taxi with his Good Samaritan after cajoling the taxi driver to follow him to his compound by flashing a sizeable wad of cash under his nostrils.

At his villa, over a glass of Limoncello, Abatelli and Wengchan became familiar with each other, the capo learning about the other man's wish to go to America. He also happily discovered Wengchan's budding proficiency with basic foreign-language skills, including Italian and English–a sought-after skillset among the American businessmen with whom he worked on international interests. To Wengchan's good fortune, Abatelli shared enough information about the Mafia business he conducted to whet Wengchan's appetite. He added that he would set up an introduction to meet his American counterpart, Victor Molinari, in New York City, perhaps calculating that this

Chinese man's skills might come in handy one day.

Wengchan did not deliberate over the offer. After a decade of hard labor on the docks, he opted for a change of venue and a different line of work, "I can meet."

* * *

Abatelli and Molinari, on the phone, discussing Wengchan and the first interview in Italy, realized his profile fit their concept of the ideal contract man: someone who could and would do their bidding in strict anonymity at any time and in any place. If he ever betrayed their loyalty or by his action, their trust, eliminating him would be possible without much concern about revved up government attention or intervention. They understood that he was not, like them, an Italian, nor was he an American. Moreover, because the communists took over in China and forced his departure from his motherland, Wengchan was a "Man Without a Country"—the *consummate* candidate for what they had in mind!

However, the two capos missed or ignored one glaring, salient point about Wengchan: an untraceable man without loyalties—no country, no conscience, no emotional ties—possessed the potential to make things messy for them if he ever felt wronged!

Several days later, on board a cruise liner steaming across the Atlantic to New York harbor, Wengchan anticipated his new work and arranged for a name change and official papers to establish a new identity for himself. The unique name he developed, he thought, would be more acceptable to the Italian Mafia; thus, China's expatriate Wengchan Liang became Peter Wei!

Upon Wei's arrival, an underling of Molinari greeted him on American soil. The escort took him to an apartment in Chinatown that Molinari had chosen for him.

After a few days of settling in, Wei began a series of regular bodybuilding exercises between outdoor ventures around Manhattan. He soaked up the city's culture in libraries and museums and familiarized himself with Manhattan's different ethnic sectors. Inside his apartment, he embraced work-related self-study and skill drills as he waited for the call from the man who could be his new employer.

Weeks after discreetly surveilling his newcomer through his hidden network of spies, Victor "The Mole" Molinari summoned him to his nearby Little Italy office on Mulberry Street.

Wei arrived prepared to discuss his terms for employment and the rules of engagement vis-a-vis Molinari.

CHAPTER 6: THE MOLE

Victor Molinari's prepubescent years ran through the Thirties. After the deaths of his parents, he maneuvered through a rough-and-tumble childhood in a depressing time of lost fortunes, no wages, rampant unemployment, and long soup lines made up of decent people down on their luck. The devil-may-care largesse and national exuberance of the Roaring Twenties, in part a resurgence of renewed hope after World War I, had ended almost overnight on the sour note of a busted stock market, shuttered banks, and unemployment shock across the nation.

The teenager Molinari, whose mother Filomena earlier died from tuberculosis, drifted in and out of street-corner gangs composed of young toughies who used back alleys as their turf for activities that brought in whatever money was good for the getting (or taking)! He had scrapes with law enforcement, but not because his Grandmother Amelia Molinari was lax on discipline at home; she was Old Country tough. When the Spanish Flu killed her husband a decade earlier, she took over management of the basic-needs store he left behind. That responsibility trapped most of her days and evenings and was her primary income source to shelter and feed herself and her young charge. Left with no other choice than praying that he would survive the streets, she let her grandson fend for himself between the cracks like a weed in a minefield laced with lethal dangers: one wrong step, a wrong turn, and he was dead.

Victor owed his nickname (The Mole) to his grandfather's legacy, which, in part, included a rather large mole on his left cheek near his upper lip. Aside from the genetic blemish, his looks were average but certainly not worthy of ridicule. When Grandmother Molinari caught wind of the rumor that others bullied her grandson in elementary school classrooms and playgrounds, she sat him down. She explained how her husband had survived similar gauntlets.

"Victor, your grandfather never let words or references to his birthmark bother him. He thought of it as a play on the proud Molinari family name. So, don't you go worrying about that. You'll get over it. Trust me."

Within her field of vision, he accepted that explanation and acted the part, but he silently vowed to exact his revenge on the worst offenders who constantly made him feel bad or fear for his life. The older he grew, and the more abuse he took, the better his vengeful plan gelled inside his brain. He took on boxing lessons, honing his skills inside the local gym after school. Sharpened to his liking, he sought out and punched the kids that he targeted, besting each opponent with one swift roundhouse right straight into their faces, in most cases breaking their jaws, shutting down their callous remarks forever!

Vindicated in the mirror, Molinari came to *like* his street-fighting name and his genetic mark so much that he used the title to introduce himself to others.

"Nice to meet you. I'm Victor 'The Mole' Molinari. You got a problem with that?!"

The smart ones right away accepted whatever he told them and never looked directly at Molinari's birthmark. Others who stared at it suffered declines in their health!

Aware that he was a one-person band longing to be part of a group where he could shine, Molinari decided to become a made-man for the Manhattan Mob and vowed to somehow enter through his grandmother's business.

The Molinari retail shop had a perfect "hideaway" room behind the dry goods stored in the back. When alive, his grandfather groomed and perfected the space for his side business. Like most living and working on the Lower East Side at the time, he, too, ran the numbers. And when he died, his widow picked up the slack. She kept running with the same customers to help make ends meet. However, she never would have escalated activity out of the backroom if not for an unusual offer she accepted one day, feeling that it was one she could not refuse.

On the day of her husband's interment, standing amid a cluster of Elm trees under umbrellas warding off raindrops softly falling on the first green grasses of spring, several local Mob capos gathered around the grieving widow and offered their condolences. One by one, they peeled off, leaving only two.

Paying their respects, the remaining two capos urged the widow to accept their offer to use her shop's backroom as a numbers drop-off location and stop demanding protection payments from her. They would let her keep her small-numbers operation.

Observing the capo's cat-and-mouse routine, young Victor, keenly aware of the game they were running on the helpless woman, *liked* it! He vowed to make what they did his career, promising himself that he would run it better than they and maybe one day take over!

After making his bones with a favor, Victor rapidly rose in Mafia rankings. He took over as the local capo in charge of the numbers-racket crew on the Lower East Side, a second-generation position for him because his father had been the first lineage who worked within the mob's domestic rank and file. Molinari Senior would have been proud to see what his boy accomplished; however, his life ended during a turf-war battle years earlier.

Molinari found the Mob world rewarding and intriguing. He expanded his influence rapidly and attempted to forge solid relations with other capos who controlled WB, believing the connection would someday work to his advantage as a man with a broad mission and the ability to better the status quo. To that end, he also made connections with police detectives "under the table" and only with individuals amenable to bribes. However, the implicit rule among Mafia was to never make contact with or mingle with any law-and-order officials unless sanctioned from above. The reason for the law was obvious: each made-man had to have 100-percent certainty who was loyal and who was not. Capos and soldiers alike preferred to know that each member respected this mandate under penalty of mayhem or death.

When Victor Molinari received word from Lorenzo Abatelli in Italy about Wengchan Liang, he wanted to meet the unusual man to size him up in person. He already had a position in mind for the new man from China!

CHAPTER 7: WEI'S COVER

As Wei walked the short distance from his apartment in Chinatown to the Felsina Social Club in Little Italy to meet Molinari, he noticed two made-men sitting in front of the club's location. Closer now, he and they watched a car pull into a parking space in front of the club. A well-dressed man and woman exited the vehicle. The gentleman prepared to drop coins into the parking meter when one of the club's onlookers stopped him.

"Hey, forget that. Are you taking your lady to dinner?"

The man nodded as his lady watched and waited.

"No need to put your money in the meter; we'll watch your car."

Hesitant at first to accept the offer, he replied, "Why, thank you very much."

Observing this interaction, Wei marveled at how much influence The Mole wielded in Little Italy.

That done, the other of the two made-men saw that Wei was approaching the Club's entrance, "You here to see Victor?"

"Yes."

"We were told to look out for you. You go right in."

His partner corroborated the invitation, "You meet with the Boss, you go right in. How long you gonna be, a couple of hours?"

"Less."

"No sweat. Go! You're covered, and so are they," he said, pointing in the direction of the couple walking away arm in arm toward nearby Pasquale's Restaurant.

Before Wei could respond to the men, one of them shifted slightly, and a flash of sunlight glinted off the piece he had under his jacket. He took that as another sign of assurance that he was in the right place.

The meeting between Molinari and Wei went down like butter. The overall tone was one of professional courtesy after a jittery first round with each man verbally tiptoeing around the other, poking and probing for strengths and weaknesses like two pugilists inside a canvas ring.

Molinari opened with a short jab, “You Peter Wei?”

Wei jabbed back, “Yes.”

“You from China?”

“Yes, China.”

“I’ve never been outside of Manhattan except to Coney Island. You know where that is?”

“No.”

“I gotta take you there sometime, get you some frankfurters with mustard and ‘kraut on a fresh bun.”

“I vegetarian.”

“Too bad for you. Nathan’s are *delizioso*! The best in the world!”

“I take word.”

Round one ended in a draw, but they had a lot of business to cover, and they soon warmed to each other.

"Wei, are you good for your word?"

"I never betray before. Why I betray you?"

"Good answer, Wei. I like that. You want a drink of something?"

"Green tea?"

"Green tea?! I was thinking of something a lot stronger, Wei."

"In your position, hard good. For me, no alcohol better."

"Another good answer. You need a steady trigger finger, right?"

"I like breathe."

Molinari, not knowing how to respond to that, laughed nervously.

"Well, Wei, you've arrived with your reputation about your knife skills preceding you. I hear you saved my friend's ass in Italy."

"I help man in trouble."

"That's what we do, Wei; we help people in trouble. The store owners around here pay us for protection, and we take care of them; you interested?"

"Need work, yes."

"Good, because I'm offering you a position as a 'cleaner.'" You know what that is, Wei?"

"Mr. Molinari, I know guns and how use them. I know fight from war. I not take orders. I work alone. You give contract, and I clean mess. Yes, I know cleaner."

"Impressive, Wei. I like your style. You're hired if you want the position. You'll also need a day job, so let's have you assist me in my numbers operation. Let me explain.

"The 'Italian Lottery' or 'Number's Racket,' as we like to call it in this country, is based on the last three digits of the amount bettors place on a specific race day at the horse track, published in New York newspapers. Bettors (gamblers, as we call them) place bets with a bookie. They do this at all types of locations—bars, social clubs, taverns, or retail stores. Gamblers' bets are guesses of what the three numbers might be at the end of the day. Runners work for the bookies. They carry the bets and the money to the main headquarters;

mine is on the Lower East Side. I belong to the Gallucci family, which runs the numbers racket in the whole country. Chinatown and Little Italy are my territories.

"A bettor wins, and we pay about 600 to 1, which you ain't gonna find anywhere. The rest of the money taken in goes to pay the bookies, the runners, and, of course, myself. What's left goes to the big man in charge of all numbers in this country, Joey 'Gap' Gaporini, working for the Gallucci Family out of his headquarters in Williamsburg Brooklyn. Sometimes you will hear Joey referred to as 'Gap,' a nickname he got from the space between his front teeth; it's a play on his name like mine, 'The Mole.' *Capische*?

"You need number collector, number runner, that right?"

"Exactly! And for your cover, we have several Chinese laundry locations that are betting places. I'm gonna assign you to pick up money and betted numbers there, and you bring what you collect to my headquarters at the end of every day."

"I understand. I take job."

Wei shook his head affirmatively. Once.

Molinari accepted the gesture as a sign that their gentlemen's agreement was now active. Cordiality prevailed as they worked out more details of the terms of service. Wei agreed to run the numbers according to rules laid down by Molinari, but on cleaning gigs, he would be autonomous about how and when he terminated his targets. In turn, Molinari vowed to cover his back so long as he produced and kept matters "clean and tidy."

Once outside the club by way of the back entrance, Wei walked to the alley's end and turned onto the main street. He tapped his fedora brim ever so slightly in the direction of the same two made-men sitting at the club's entrance. They nodded back and watched as he walked past and out of sight.

"The Boss must see something in dat guy!" one said to the other.

"How should I know? I never seen him do business with a Chinese before."

"Looks like it. The guy sure must have some special skills!"

"Hey Goombah, what's your special skill?"

"Sittin' on my big fat ass watching this joint!"

"Yeah, Goombah! That's why we're outside sitting here on the sidewalk, and he was inside."

"Yeah, you got that right, but I'm happy. You happy?"

"Yeah, I'm happy 'cause there's never gonna be no guns aimed at my head!"

* * *

Wei's secret life never interfered with his double-layered cover: daytime presser in one of the Chinese laundries. He labored under Molinari's umbrella when not tasked to run numbers. The circle of co-workers who worked side by side with Wei only knew that he came and went at odd times, especially when their manager handed him a slip of paper that looked a lot like a short laundry list. When not for a collection run, the sheets meant a cleanup.

When Wei left his worksite, others surmised that he could be gone for days or weeks at a time; they never knew why, but they knew better than to ask.

Of course, none of this activity was tabloid news, table-gossip fodder across WB dining-room tables, or a topic for discussion in darkened alleys in Manhattan's Chinatown—Ground Zero for a Chinese Mafia yet to come.

Wei worked alone. He and his employer preferred it that way. Still, he was never "lonely" because memories of his parents' deaths—signal flares in his life that never dimmed—were constant companions reminding him every waking hour that silence was golden.

Anonymous, skilled perfection was the only guarantee for his survival!

Everyone required income to survive, and Wei's life was no exception. As he wished to live a long life, he held two rules as his stable data: be truer and more professional than your peers, and build a reserve of cash large enough to enable walking away whenever the emotional toll became unbearable.

Relief from his work, he knew, would always be a fleeting mistress. Travel was his counterbalance. He liked to vacation far from his work's harsh realities, including, as often as needed, visits to his new friend, Lorenzo Abatelli. Taking solace wherever he could find it in Abatelli's company or outside in the country, he drew and painted landscapes *al fresco*—whatever would transport his mind back to the innocent days of his early childhood on the farm.

Wei felt at home living in Chinatown and within the mixed bag of nationalities that made up the Lower East Side. His secluded residence, a loft on Pell Street, abutted a darkened and abandoned opium den. From there, every awake hour when not on a job, he spent in the gym he had set up for himself. Beyond honing his body, he further developed his craft by experimenting with various disguises, assembling false identities with matching credentials, and adding to his admirable array of weaponry that comprised his repertoire. He used each piece until he perfected his skills and certainty about his level of practical proficiency with it.

Mentally aware of his work's intricacies, Wei wrote meticulous notes on which he outlined various scenarios that he might find himself in and multiple options for extricating himself from each to maximize his probability for survival. Longevity, he knew, depended on his winning every time. Failure meant death.

Although Wei and Gap never met, Gap noticed Wei's demonstrated record of impeccable competence over time. As a result, Molinari got a call from Gap, asking to let him use Wei to help with his numbers operation in WB. For cover, Molinari assigned Wei to work at the Chinese laundry located on Conselyea behind the Chichi's restaurant parking lot, a block past Lorimer and merely a few doors away from Angie Carpello's stoop.

Gap assigned a handler, a made-man, to shadow Wei, charging him to observe him, size him up, verify his actions and whereabouts without Wei ever suspecting, and evaluate how he could best benefit Gap's operation. Stevie "Snots" Matteo's ruddy skin underlay light brown hair haloed around a balding patch on top. His oval-shaped face and skin were smooth and unblemished. He commanded a manly look, except that his two eyes set closer than most other people. His signature habit, constant snorting nasal inhalations from a congenital septum problem, earned him his nickname. Yet, those who knew him or worked with him liked Snots for his unquestioned loyalty. A dyed-in-the-wool team player, he grew up in WB, the only son of immigrant parents from Nola, Italy.

Wei preferred to take his breaks up in the office above the laundry. From there, he could observe in complete anonymity every movement made in the parking lot below. He noted the Mafiosos who dined in Chichi's and learned the regular traffic patterns and daily schedules of every regular visitor, including the Mafia soldiers who appeared near the bar and restaurant doorways whenever capos and bosses held meetings inside Chichi's.

Wei went about his assigned tasks, and Snots duly observed his activities. Simultaneously, the reigning Mafia bosses on both sides of the East River kept alive the habits of their Old-Country Italian bosses by obeying the timeless roots and immutable principles of the culture that ran through their bloodstreams like extra-virgin olive oil.

When Gap and Molinari considered Wei ready for the primary task they had in mind right from their first phone discussion about him, they never could have imagined the cards which Fate would deal to each of them. Treason from an unexpected enemy, a traitor within their ranks, would eventually have them turning to Wei to handle a task so sensitive that the life or death of their entire Manhattan and WB operations would hang on his success!

Nor could they know that the path on which their work and their survival depended would lead straight to a girl growing up close by in WB, Angelina Carpello.

CHAPTER 8: WHERE TO DINE?

Luigi's wife and two daughters were finishing their delicious slices of pie and licking from their fingers the last remnants when he stepped outside and joined them on the stoop, announcing that he intended to take his family out for dinner Saturday evening. Instantly, he received enthusiastic hugs and kisses that left pie-filling scraps on his cheeks just beyond the wide smile spread across his face.

Chichi's Restaurant was the Carpello family's favorite. Family members had dined there for decades. Angie's Grandparents, Giuseppe and Gabriella, ate there in the Twenties when it was just a tavern. Today, Luigi visited Chichi's daily to have a beer or two with friends, at times also continuing to bartend there on weekends. On Wednesdays, after he picked up his daughters from school around one o'clock PM—the early time allowed public school children to go to religious instruction classes at Angie's and JJ's elementary school—he took his girls there for lunch. In turn, they looked forward to this outing with their dad, often ordering their favorites, plates of soppressata and provolone cheese, followed by a dish of Pasta Fagioli made with assorted kinds of pasta and chopped prosciutto. Beyond the food, the girls' greatest treats were playing songs they liked on the jukebox and ordering Shirley Temple drinks with *three* Maraschino cherries in each glass, not one—they also snuck behind the bar and snatched more cherries when no one was looking!

Chichi's, being so near to the Carpello's house, practically right across the street, was the easiest place for the Carpellos to dine in since they could walk there in minutes and enjoy an unhurried meal. Angie and JJ usually chattered with each other about what they might select from the menu, JJ savoring the fried shrimp, and Angie teasing her about her selection because she thought everyone should eat something 'Italian' at an Italian restaurant. JJ never minded her sister's remarks and stuck with her shrimp choice every time; on the other hand, Angie always ordered the ravioli. Caterina selected linguine with clams in oil and garlic, and Luigi, willing to try something different on each visit, consistently called for the Chef's Special.

Mindful of certain fellow diners thought to be Mafia bosses—in fact, themselves simply hungry customers, the Carpellos dined at Chichi's several times a year on Sundays and, of course, all holidays. The whole family, distant relatives included, loved the food and the diverse atmosphere. One time, Aunt Rosa Maria was already there when the Carpellos arrived for dinner. She sat with Dominic Chichi's wife, Lucia, and his sister, Joyce, a nun in the Catholic Dominican Order. A few tables away, Dominic's mistress Giulia and their son, who looked exactly like him, were eating their dinners. None but those who paid close attention to stoop gossip ever knew that tangled web of related connections!

Therefore, for several reasons, Chichi's would have been Luigi's and the girls' primary choice of where to dine Saturday evening, except that an unexpected, bizarre incident altered their plans the night before around midnight.

After the Carpellos and their neighbors had retired for the night, the entire block awoke to the ominous sounds of multiple vehicles screeching to a halt, squad car lights flashing, the smell of smoke in the air, and the escalating blare of sirens from the direction of the local firehouse. Angie, JJ, Luigi, and Caterina rushed out of bed and to the front door. Stepping outside onto the stoop, they saw most of their neighbors standing outside in their bedclothes and robes, watching flames shoot out of the windows of Chichi's kitchen. A blockade of unmarked cars and traffic officers re-directed traffic at the corner.

As the first fire engines pulled up, adding more color and pressurized streams of water to the already flashy scene, a handful of plainclothes detectives led by their sergeant, Detective Daniel Scarpelli, arrived and surveyed the grounds surrounding the restaurant. Scarpelli, taking care first to put protective gloves on his hands, turned, unnoticed, toward the kitchen side door and entered the smoldering ruins.

Not a single soul suspected that Scarpelli also worked on Molinari's side and knew all about the numbers racket run out of Chichi's, including the bookies' names associated with the operation. Those details getting into the wrong hands would collapse his main source of moonlighting income, so he was not about to let anyone else discover them amid the chaos of the fire and water or the inevitable scouring search for evidence of the fire's origin.

Moving quickly once inside the kitchen—firefighters and other officials had not yet declared the building safe to enter—Scarpelli grabbed every betting-numbers sheet and list of names he could find, those that were not entirely burnt. What remained he stuffed into his pockets before slipping back outside to the topsy-turvy scene—a decidedly successful, undetected reconnaissance run! His inside knowledge guaranteed complete success at removing all lists and numbers while escaping any suspicion of complicity or guilt. Because of his police force status and position on the Mafia payroll, he thought *I have all the cover I need.*

* * *

"Girls, get away from the door and go back to bed," ordered Luigi, concerned that they would see more than they should.

The sisters, in turn, laughed and begged him to stay until the excitement dissipated. He insisted they return to bed and go to sleep, and off they went.

Word on the street suggested that one of the chefs accidentally burned some food while cooking, notwithstanding the severity of the flames the residents witnessed before the firefighters arrived. Of course, those neighbors on the block, who knew better, returned to bed for whatever time they had left to get rested before the crack of dawn.

Luigi woke up still determined to treat his family to a nice dinner someplace. At the Carpello breakfast table, the family talked over where they might like to dine. Since Chichi's was out due to the ongoing investigation, the family agreed to eat at nearby Milo's after much back and forth.

Milo's Restaurant, located on Lorimer Street between Devoe Street and Metropolitan

Avenue, only two blocks from the Carpello family home, was a good spot for pizza, scungilli, or Capozzelle (roasted lamb's head—Angie's favorite). But Milo's had a reputation.

Counterpointing the excellent food prepared and served there, patrons regularly referred to Milo's as the "Bucket of Blood" because of an unfortunate incident associated with the restaurant's location. Due to his daughters' young ages, Luigi declined to explain when one of the girls brought up the subject, saying it did not matter.

Milo's operated inside the lower-level, first floor of a row house. Next to the restaurant's entrance, steps led to the structure above the eatery. One day, legend had it that some young, adult men sat and chatted on the stoop for some time and then stood up and departed, leaving one of them behind with an ice pick stuck in his ear. His blood trickled down his torso and the stoop stairs before a waiter discovered the murder. The horrific incident, par for the course within certain WB circles at the time, handed the popular restaurant a timeless and infamous legacy that seemed to last forever, and the establishment stayed alive only because of the quality of its food!

Was the unfortunate incident too messy to qualify as a Mafia hit? Was it a sophomoric attempt to impress someone, an indiscriminate rite-of-passage, or simply an argument's poor outcome?

Difficult to prove, the real answer likely went to someone's grave in Williamsburg Brooklyn.

CHAPTER 9: PROTECTION

With the gravy for the Sunday dinner prepared, Caterina suggested to her girls that all three go outside and sit on the stoop to take advantage of the sunny weather.

They engaged in small talk about food and friends until a loud argument commenced across the street, interrupting them. Looking in the direction of the unwelcome noise, all three watched a young woman get backhanded and cursed out by a slightly older man who seemed to be her boyfriend. Caterina took the scene as her cue to teach her girls an important lesson.

"Girls, do you see what's happening across the street? Never allow anyone to abuse you like that. Not from any man or anyone, for that matter."

Their eyes stayed glued to the scene as it unfolded before them, their ears perked, listening.

"You're each getting older now. You must be careful who you speak to and with whom you make friends. Do you hear me, girls?!" Caterina repeated a bit more energetically, intending that they look at her.

The girls nodded and turned toward her.

"A lot goes on in this neighborhood that I'm sure you're aware of, so, at all times, you must watch out for yourselves and each other, okay?"

Angie brazenly responded, "Don't worry, mom. I can take care of myself and will protect my sister!"

Caterina reacted by reminding them that there was good and bad in everyone and that even though they lived in a safe neighborhood, they still had to be careful, "... Because, sometimes, people you know can be your worst enemies."

* * *

Any adult in WB could casually observe the American Mafia's obvious presence. Because of their ages, Angie and JJ were only now coming to some understanding of its organized nature. Throughout the few years of their lives, there had been signs. Residents, relatives, friends, and guests of all ages, sitting on WB stoops, often watched the familiar pattern of Mob-related activities unfold right before their eyes. Mafia bosses reserved every Wednesday night for business meetings at Chichi's, their anointed gathering spot a mere three row houses away from Angie's stoop. On those evenings, a veritable parade of Cadillacs appeared at sunset and continued through the night. Their occupants parked them on Conselyea Street, Lorimer Street, or Chichi's reserved lot next to the Chinese laundry.

Mafia business gatherings were, for the most part, routine and quiet affairs. However, one or two wise guys stood watch without fail outside any night that key personnel gathered. Participants in the meetings usually sat with their backs to the interior wall at the dining room's largest corner table. These conclaves consisted of capos with major social and influence status within the organization.

The mid-week gatherings complemented regular Friday-night dinners when made-men accompanied their mistresses. On Saturday nights, their wives sat next to them!

That was the way it was at Chichi's.

* * *

Caterina and her girls were still sitting on the stoop when Joey Gap parked his Cadillac right in front of them near the fire hydrant. Stepping out on his own, he saw the two girls and addressed their mother, *"Caterina, Buon Giorno."*

"Grazie, buon appetito," she responded warmly.

"Prego," answered Gap, who already had turned and was walking by himself toward Chichi's.

Angie and JJ followed with their eyes, noticing his neat attire consisting of a dark jack shirt and pressed slacks. He walked confidently and crisply to the restaurant's side entrance. There, greeted by a capo who seemed to know him well, he disappeared inside.

Caterina harbored no special opinion about the other Mobsters. Still, she respected Gap, who always acted like a gentleman and was often helpful to people she knew in the WB neighborhood.

Caterina, a devout Catholic actively engaged with the Shrine of the Madonna Church as a congregation member and volunteer, could be found often at events sponsored by the St. Rita's Society, Italian Heritage Association, and Knights of Columbus Ladies Auxiliary. When a new pastor, Father Andrew Conti, arrived at the venerable church, he became acquainted with her volunteerism. One Sunday after Mass, he spoke to her in confidence, sharing that he had noticed that every week two men working for the Mafia took a cut of the church's collected donations.

Of course, Caterina was surprised to hear this was happening. Emboldened by the pastor's confidence in her, she told Father Conti that she knew someone to whom she could speak about the situation, who probably would help.

Conti gave Caterina his official blessing to meet with that person and determine what he could do to assist them.

Before long, sitting with Joey Gap at Chichi's bar Caterina explained her proposition: "We have a new Pastor, Father Conti, and he wants to do what's best for the church and its parishioners. I think you will agree with me that all of the money should be going to the church."

"I will look into it," was all Gap told her as he graciously led her out and bid her goodbye.

The following Sunday, ushers passed the collection baskets from pew to pew during each Mass. This time nothing out of the ordinary happened, and after the services, no one showed up to get a piece of the heavenly pie. Gap had stone-cold stopped that action because of Caterina's intervention.

Wizened to the ways of the centuries-old Mafia, Caterina had understood that no soldier would ever maneuver such a bold move against the church without the Gap's prior approval! She correctly surmised Gap's involvement right from the start but smartly never let on that she knew. Her feat was no small deal because "Joey Gap" Gaporini was well-connected and, as one of the

Gallucci Family's main bosses, wielded a lot of power in New York and across America.

Back on the stoop, as Angie and JJ stood up to go to Mary's Candy Store—the walk would take them past Chichi's, their budding physical changes plainly showed. Nearing the eatery, they saw Gap coincidentally step outside. He stopped at the top of the stairs and watched the sisters walk arm in arm toward him.

He exchanged hellos, adding a compliment, "You're growin' up into such lovely ladies. If anyone should bother any of you in any way, you let me know, okay?"

The girls, a little startled and a little celebrity-shy thanked him politely but walked on at a faster pace, thinking they were safer that way.

Unknown to them, Gap, for good measure, looked back toward the Carpello's stoop and, leaning forward, waved to Caterina, putting on an air of decorum for her sake, which she barely noticed since she was looking after her daughters.

To Angie, knowing safety and feeling safe were two separate, indefinite and barely understood notions. She understood that they lived in a protected neighborhood but often felt uneasy after witnessing as she grew up with scores of ruthless incidents around her.

Like Angie, the vast majority of people living and working in WB wanted only a safe environment in which to discover, express, and enjoy simple pleasures and raise their families as close as possible to cherished family traditions developed in the Old Country! And, of course, to live the American Dream of knowing that their offspring and future generations would live and survive in a better world than theirs.

CHAPTER 10: REMINISCENCE

Sunday traffic on Conselyea was light, almost non-existent. A pale blue sky embraced wispy, white cloud puffs that would later morph into orange and mauve hues at the onset of another sunset. The chill and slush of winter were still a couple of months away.

Coming into her age of puberty and sitting alone on her stoop after the Sunday-afternoon dinner, Angie thought, as she had all week, about certain enigmas in her life and where they might lead her. She was keenly aware of the physical, mental, and emotional changes happening to her without having all the answers to them. For now, though, the silence and softness of the hour, and the freedom of her privacy, satisfied her. She felt contented.

Full from Caterina's typical Sunday meal: antipasto of prosciutto, soppressata, genoa salami, capocollo, mozzarella, provolone, and assorted black and green olives, multiple servings of Rigatoni macaroni with sausage, meatballs, and braciole in the gravy, and capped off with roasted chicken, sauteed spinach and a tossed salad, some of the relatives had earlier decided to take a long walk and return later for some nuts, fruits, pastries, and a cup or two of espresso. Angie, therefore, had the stoop all to herself. Feeling peaceful, she focused her mind on her future, bringing her to consider her Aunt Sofia's musical talents, thinking that she might want to pursue a career in music.

Sofia loved to sing. She was a natural soprano. As a young girl, she performed in the church choir every Sunday at Mass, displaying a standout talent that other people easily noticed. Troubling her, Sofia's immediate family lacked enthusiasm for her to attend a prestigious music school and have a career in music. Consequently, Sofia auditioned at the Juilliard School of Music, thinking that her opportunity would be nothing more than a hopeless tryout without her family's support. To her surprise, she won the panel of judges' backing, and they awarded her a partial scholarship! Sharing the good news with her astonished parents, she pleasantly discovered that she had their support. They even assured her that somehow they would find a way to pay the rest of her tuition!

Once enrolled, Sofia thought that she would be looked down upon by her peers and the older students. On the contrary, once they heard her sing, she quickly found them actively supportive. Egging her on past her fears throughout her initial semester, they assisted her with her studies and homework. When research required that she learn and practice various piano pieces to pass each audible exam performance requirement, she found ready help from her friends.

After graduation, Sofia's singing career blossomed. She sang at Carnegie Hall and appeared on the *Arthur Godfrey Show*. Several talent agents pursued her. The world was becoming her oyster until she decided that working as a professional musician did not suit her personality.

Sofia's personal decision never diminished her love for the art or her enthusiasm. She passed both on to her niece, Angie, who took piano lessons from age seven and, a bit later, discovered the guitar, an instrument she kept learning and practicing without fail.

Opening and sweeping her eyes across the colorful fall scene before her, Angie felt serene. She thought about how much she enjoyed performing with others in her guitar group at the church's Saturday Night Folk Mass. And how, as a member of the Madonna of the Shrine Cadet Corps with JJ and her two friends, sisters Francesca and Anna Maria Panarelli, she played the snare and bass drums with Francesca, while Anna Maria and JJ played the fife.

As a kaleidoscope of images continued to roll through Angie's mind, she wished her grandmother were still alive, and she remembered spending every moment she could with her from infancy. Returning to the time she was 13 months old—a story told anecdotally to her, Angie recalled her grandmother's move to Miami with Rosa Maria to establish legal residency there so her daughter could file for divorce. Back then, by law, New York divorces involved proof of adultery, and in her situation, that was not the case.

When her parents watched their daughter grow melancholic, they surmised that missing her grandmother's caring heart and presence was the cause. Soon after, little Angie and Caterina boarded the Silver Star train headed to Miami and a reunion that, hopefully, would renew her happiness.

Reunited, Angie and her grandmother spent days at the beach, swimming in the pool and happily eating frankfurters hot off the barbecue grill. After two weeks, Caterina and her rejuvenated infant traveled home, secure in the knowledge that it would not be long before grandmother would return, too.

For Angie, the pleasant memory was too brief. Her mood changed, and she felt renewed pangs from an earlier emotional setback upon recalling her grandmother's passing.

Oh, how I miss her so! As soon as I could crawl out of my crib, I would go upstairs and get into bed with my grandparents every morning. And breakfast was always a poached egg and toast with butter prepared for me by my grandmother.

Thinking of the foods that she shared with her grandmother rearranged Angie's mood again and pushed her memories to better times spent among her extended family.

We were a close family. My grandparents always had relatives and friends visiting. I loved the excitement of everybody enjoying our time together, chatting, gossiping, and eating, always eating!

Satisfied, Angie giggled and smiled to herself just as the dinner party returned from their walk. Waving to Angie as they passed her, they went back inside the house. Permitted to revel in a few more thoughts, she laughed and remembered her late grandfather.

Sometimes after dinner, while the family sat on the stoop and he sat next to me, he would get "La Voglia," a craving for a certain type of food. Yelling to my father, he stood up and declared, "Luigi, go get the car, and let's go to Coney Island for some Nathan's Frankfurters." Other times, he yelled, "Let's go have clams on a half shell at Lundy's in Sheepshead Bay!" Or "C'mon, Luigi, let's go to Juniors for cheesecake."

And away we all went, stuffed in the car with whoever had stopped by to sit on the stoop. I enjoyed going to Lundy's Restaurant. I could sit at the bar and eat two dozen Little Necks all by myself!

Next to return were more thoughts of how her grandmother had meant everything to her: *Grandma went to the beauty parlor every week to get her hair styled, taking me in tow. As the dresser styled her hair, I sat in the big chair and got a manicure. We both left feeling pretty good about ourselves. And on the way home, we usually stopped at the stationery store to get a toy for me.*

"How sad..." she said aloud, standing up and stretching after another random thought crept out, making her feel like it was only yesterday: "... and how uncanny that Grandfather Pietro disowned us *after* my grandfather and grandmother passed! Maybe he was afraid of Grandpa Giuseppe? I don't know. What I do know is that when Grandma Gabriella died, all the joy left the house!"

At that moment, Caterina called out through the open window, "Angie, come inside to have some nuts, fruits, and pastries!"

Angie stretched again and went inside to rejoin the family for dessert.

❖

CHAPTER 11: FRIENDS FOR THE SIXTIES

Angie's favorite friend Francesca, though a year younger and blonde-haired and blue-eyed, was pure Italian. The two friends consistently spent hours together, playing one game or another outdoors. Almost every day, they were at Macri Triangle Park on Union and Conselyea adjacent to the Brooklyn-Queens Expressway. Although little more than a sandlot surrounded by trees, the whole area became a field suitable for games of catch once the adventurous girls climbed up and jumped over the iron fence on its perimeter. Other times, games of stickball were possible with teams made up from scratch with different friends.

For now, with no one else around to bother them, the two girlfriends pounded their baseball gloves and threw a "Spaldeen" ball in a game of catch accented by whatever topic of conversation was on their minds.

"What time is everyone else coming?" Francesca asked Angie.

"In about ten minutes. Tom invited a friend of his to play stickball with us."

"Well, I hope we have an even number of players so we can all play."

They continued in silence; the only sounds the ball hitting the sweet spots in the pockets of each glove and the traffic speeding past on the adjacent expressway.

Breaking the silence, Francesca commented, "How about that guy getting beat up on our block last week?!"

"You mean when we were playing stoop ball?"

"Yeah. That was scary!"

"You're telling me! I can still see that man getting out of his car, and those two mean guys punching the daylights out of him!"

Francesca kept it going, "The victim sure seemed pretty timid, but it sounded like he owed the other guys some money. It was horrible how they just kept kicking him."

The thought silenced both girls for several minutes until once again Francesca broke the ice, "The best part, though, was your mother coming outside to tell us to get inside, and you having none of that."

"Well, I wasn't going to stop a good game just because some guy was getting beat up. Conselyea's my block, our block, too! Besides, I was ahead of you at that point!"

Francesca laughed at her friend, "Well, it's a good thing they stopped and walked away because if they hadn't, *I* would have punched you out and dragged you inside of your house myself to get you away from them!"

Speechless, Angie dropped the ball coming at her.

Francesca filled in the void, "When I said that scene scared me, you said you were scared, too, but why didn't you listen to your mom and go inside?"

"For some reason, all I could think of was, *why do I have to stop playing stoop ball and go inside just because three men that I never saw before were fighting over money across the street?"*

They would have to pick up the subject later because Tom's arrival with two friends, Sal and Valentina, a twosome from Greenpoint, diverted their attention.

There weren't enough of them to make up two evenly staffed teams, so the players took turns hitting while the others took on defensive positions in the field.

About an hour and a couple of "spaldeens" lost to traffic later, a few of the players called it a game. Crossing Union Avenue, they headed for Jerry's Candy Store. They ordered egg creams, the iconic drink created around 1900 by Louis Auster, a Jewish immigrant and a Lower East Side candy shop owner. He invented the venerated drink by mixing fresh whole milk, bottled seltzer, and Fox's U-Bet chocolate syrup—and frankfurters smothered in mustard and sauerkraut as they sat down.

Angie and Francesca sat next to each other in the same booth as Sal and Valentina. Never having met before, they learned that they attended Saint Theresa's Elementary School, a mere ten-block walk up Meeker Avenue from Macri Triangle Park.

"How do you know Tommy?" asked Francesca.

Sal answered, "I met him at a pick-up game in McCarren Park a couple of weeks ago. He invited me to play stickball with all of you today, and I brought my girlfriend."

"Yeah, when Tommy asked me to come along, I thought it would be fun to play stickball and meet new people at the same time. I'm happy we did."

Looking at Francesca and Angie for some reaction, she asked, "So, what school do you go to?"

Francesca replied, "We go to the Shrine of the Madonna School, a couple of blocks from here."

"Oh, the one that has the Italian Feast every year! My family and I have attended since I was a little kid!"

"Well, this year, maybe we can all go together and get sausage and pepper sandwiches," Angie added.

"Sounds good to me!" Francesca exclaimed, nodding along with Valentina and Sal.

"You both have to come by more often, especially you, Valentina, to play a game of stoop ball with us girls," Angie offered.

Turning, Francesca added, "Sorry, Sal, girls-only."

Sal shrugged and kept eating.

Valentina smiled and replied, "I would like that."

Angie and Valentina exchanged phone numbers to keep in touch and make plans to get together sometime.

Angie and Sal, progressing from one subject to another, gradually realized they both took guitar lessons at the same music shop on Grand Street.

Amazed, Angie commented, "Hey, let's plan to play guitars together soon." Sal agreed.

After they all left Jerry's, Angie and Francesca jumped on their bikes and rode around the neighborhood, waving and smiling at everyone as they passed by their stoops. These two best friends were inseparable; if you couldn't find them at the sandlot, riding bicycles, or roller-skating, you could likely discover them playing stoop ball on Conselyea or yakking up a storm that inevitably landed on the subject of boys.

Not quite a freshman high-schooler, Angie did have a steady boyfriend, Dante, although "dates" were more like friendly hangouts, nothing formal or too deep. Dante's father owned a nearby thriving bakery, which placed his family at a middle-class lifestyle a little above Angie's. Consequently, the young man had a sufficient spending-money allowance to go along with his budding interest in developing a closer relationship with Angie.

One school-day afternoon, as Angie and Dante descended the main stairway at school, he asked her, "Would you go see the movie *Planet of the Apes* with me on Saturday? It just came out, and it's playing at the Meserole Theater."

Angie, smitten by her friend's polite request, enthusiastically replied, "Yes! And let's have some popcorn and Cokes, too!"

Saturday afternoon arrived, and they met at the bus stop on Lorimer. Boarding for the short ride to Greenpoint, they anticipated a good time. All turned out well. On their second outing, they watched *Night of the Living Dead* in a theater packed with many of their friends. After that, their mutual classmates recognized them as a couple for the rest of the school year. They hung out together until the summer when Dante went away on vacation with his family.

While apart for a month, things cooled after Dante sent a letter to Angie from the Jersey shore, which included an odd inscription written on the envelope, "Signed with a spit," instead of "... with a kiss."

Upset, she never responded.

Upon his return to WB, Dante saw her on Lorimer Street and, smiling ear-to-ear, approached, shouting, "Hey, Angie, it's so nice to see you. I'm back. I want to tell you all about my vacation. Let's get together soon!"

She wanted to react but held back, forcing Dante to ask, "What's wrong, Angie? How are you?"

Trying not to crack a smile but wanting to, she told him, "I'm mad at you, Dante. You signed the last letter you sent me '...with a spit' and not 'with a 'kiss!' That upset me very much."

Dante, inclined to laugh but knowing better not to, apologized, "Gosh, I'm sorry, Angie. I was joking around and thought you'd get a kick out of that."

"Well, I didn't..."

Dante grew sullen.

But then Angie finished her thought, "... But I do forgive you. Do you have time to buy me a soda at Mary's Candy Store?"

"Yep, let's go!"

And off they went, continuing to see each other exclusively for the rest of the year.

* * *

When JJ, a voracious reader, was not propped up with a book on her bed, she enjoyed gabfests outside on the stoop with Anna Maria while simultaneously playing Backgammon, Rummy, and War card games.

JJ, Angie, and their friends were coming into ages where their choices of fashion mattered. JJ leaned more toward girly fashion statements, and Angie preferred a tomboy look. JJ liked to wear pretty, frilly blouses with puffed sleeves and dungarees, but t-shirts and roll-cuffed dungarees suited Angie.

Anna Maria dressed similarly to her friend and, like JJ, was a real "*chiacchierone*!" The duo yapped for hours playing their myriad games, sipping homemade iced tea dubbed by Anna Maria as " 'Brown Water,' because your mom (Caterina) cannot make good, regular iced tea!"

* * *

Gaia Carnivale from Devoe Street was another close friend and a usual member of Angie's stoop-ball team. The same age as Angie, she had a welcome sense of humor and curly locks like her father. Gaia liked to wear casual outfits consisting of t-shirts tucked into four-dollar Wrangler dungarees bought on Grand Street at Simon's Clothing Store. And, like the rest of her friends, Keds or PF Flyer sneakers covered her feet.

Gaia's father grew up in WB and knew Angie's mom for a long time. After he married, he moved his family away for an extended time, chasing a work opportunity. Once back, the girls' parents realized their daughters were similar in age and demeanor. They ended up introducing the two girls and encouraging a friendship, knowing that they would be in the same elementary school class.

Despite minor differences like Gaia's tendency to act out more eccentrically than Angie, the two girls became fast friends. For one, she sometimes carried a small salt shaker with her and, whenever she got the urge, sprinkled salt on the sidewalk and mock tap-danced in front of her friends. The salt provided just enough grit that, stepped on, echoed the sounds of a tap dancer's steel-tipped shoes (given a little added imagination)! What a kick friends, family, and strangers passing by got watching her tap on the sidewalk! The best part was that her friends laughed hilariously with her but not at her.

Most young people living on the block and the surrounding neighborhood streets had designated Angie's block on Conselyea as the unofficial "neighborhood hangout." Tonight, her stoop was prominently on display, beginning with a visit from Gaia. From several yards away, seeing her friend sitting on the stoop, she yelled, "Hey, Angie, I heard a Batman film is playing at the Meserole Theater this weekend. They expect Adam West and Burt Ward to make an appearance. Do you want to go?"

"Yes, and let's tell the gang so they can come, too."

Seemingly from nowhere came a chorus of words, "We heard that! We're in, too!"

"Count me in, Angie!"

"Yeah, I'm in, too!"

"Me, too!"

Francesca, Tom, Don, and Antoinette were walking on Conselyea towards Angie's stoop. Closer now, they discussed what street game they might play tonight. Another friend, Rose, walking on the other side of the street, overheard and, crossing the street, suggested, "Let's play Ringolevio. I'm sure Pete, Dante, and Mike will be here soon, so there will be enough of us for a good game."

Upon their arrival at the stoop, Gaia hurriedly told the final additions to the group about the upcoming Batman and Robin event. Latching onto her excitement, everyone made plans to meet on the appointed day and go together to the theater.

They then started up a game of Ringolevio, which is an altered version of the old standby, Hide & Seek. After vying for who would be team captains, the group agreed on Francesca and Tommy.

The captains took turns choosing team members amid shouts of, "I wanna be on Francesca's team!" (from Antoinette) and "I want to be on Tom's team!" (from Mike). After much debate, each team ended up with the same number of players, and the game began. Tom's team scattered and hid, while Francesca's gathered on the sidewalk, counted to the predetermined number of 25, and, hitting the count limit, ran in search of the other team's members in hiding to capture and "jail" them.

Each team designated its jail location. Tom chose Angie's stoop, and Francesca selected an open space between two parked cars. All players had agreed the game would end when each team captured all of the other team's members at least one time.

The idea on the pursuing side was to latch onto someone on the opposing team, hold them, and chant, "Ringolevio, 1-2-3, 1-2-3, 1-2-3!" Breaking free at any point during this time, the "arrested" person was un-caught and once again considered free and "in-play" in the game. If the capture held up, the pursuer escorted his or her prisoner to the designated jail area. In captivity, the player was "out" of the game, but that could change.

Gaia, a fierce player, chased after the other team's members quickly and, grabbing onto Don and chanting "Ringolevio 1-2-3, 1-2-3, 1-2-3," she pushed him into her team's jail. She then went after Rose, holding her, too, and chanting even more loudly than before, “Ringolevio 1-2-3, 1-2-3, 1-2-3!” Now Francesca’s team had two captives!

Team members not caught could free fellow members languishing in jail by barging in, un-caught, tagging the captives, and shouting, "All in! All in! Free-all!", meaning that all jailed members of the team were now free again and would have to be re-captured.

Players in jail could also extend themselves beyond the jail space by forming chains by holding hands, making it easier for teammates to free them. When a free teammate grabbed hold of someone in jail, and the chain yelled, “Electricity!” a general jailbreak occurred along with an explosion of laughter followed by a scattering of bodies!

Mike sized up Angie for capture as Angie chased Pete. Elated when he grabbed Angie, he threw her in jail on her stoop. Now, Tom’s team had at least one prisoner. And so play continued; Antoinette catching Tom, who after that languished in “jail.”

Mike and Pete, the only two uncaught on Tom's team, signaling each other with eye movements, failed to pay attention to where Dante was. While they were chasing Gaia and Francesca, Dante snatched Mike and put him in jail. Capturing Pete would signal one round of the game over.

Upping the game's difficulty level, a rule that the pursuing team could not station any of their team within line of sight of the jail—a practice called "babysitting"—was still in play.

Pete, still uncaught and the only one left free on Tom's team, attempted to free Rose. As he danced around where Rose stood in jail, everyone on the opposing team cried, "Babysitting!" and, thus, were able to block his first rescue attempt.

Pete, still running around to avoid being caught, finally grabbed Rose's hand and yelled, "Electricity!" Within a split second, everyone in jail between the parked cars held hands and shouted, "Electricity," freeing all of them.

Tom's team members were all free, so play resumed and continued this night and lasted until darkness took over, and the street lamps lit up. At times, earlier matches took days to finish, making the game a favorite any time a large gathering of friends spontaneously materialized.

Tonight, as each satisfied Ringolevio player walked back to their respective houses, the upcoming Saturday movie "date" was on everyone's minds and lips.

On Saturday, the group gathered for the short bus ride to the theater. Overheard conversations covered a wide range of topics, including the recent game.

"Hey!..." Tom, one of the team captains, shouted out, "... What about that game of Ringolevio the other night! Amazing, wasn't it?! We beat your butts!"

Before anyone responded, the bus arrived, and they all boarded. Tom fixed his stare and wide grin at those who had been opposing team members.

Responding to the challenge, Team Captain Francesca retorted, "Your team was lucky. You had 'Short Pete' on your side! He snuck in between the parked cars, latched on to Rose, and created 'electricity' too easily."

"Well, that's because I knew who to pick as a team member," Tom gloated.

Pete piped up, "Hey, Tom, wait a minute. You may have picked me, but *I won* the game for our team!"

His team members hooted in agreement. The other team's members booed, matching the decibel count in reaction. As they disembarked from the bus at the theater, opposing outcries from both teams melted into laughter, the players' enthusiasm for the game and their friendships outweighing the actual outcome.

Inside the theater and seated, the crowd hushed as the house lights dimmed and the big screen lit up. With smiles on every face, their last thoughts of the game sank back into the recesses of their minds.

Later, meeting the movie stars turned out to be a real thrill for everyone, and the bus ride home was just as boisterous as the first one!

* * *

When not playing Ringolevio or stoop ball, Johnny-on-a-Pony became this group's game of choice and another way to have lots of fun, everyone laughing throughout the entire matches. In Johnny-on-a-Pony, two teams chosen had the same number of kids on each side, equal in height and weight, to ensure the game was fair. One group picked one person to stand upright with their back against the wall of a building while the rest of the team bent over with each of their heads up in someone else's butt/crotch area, forming what looked like a long horse torso. The other team then jumped, one by one, on top of the "human horse chain." Opposing players leaped up with as much force as possible, hoping to collapse the other team's invented human-horse torso. Either team member falling to the ground meant their team lost. If all opposing members sat astride the interlocked team members and no one fell, a coin toss determined who won the round. A completed round signaled a switch of team roles.

Street games were integral to growing up healthy in WB. Participating, Angie and her friends welcomed the release of daily emotional highs and lows associated with the games. Now that the Sixties were upon the nation and WB, relief was even more important.

As military-duty draft notices arrived in America's mailboxes, Angie's male friends were lucky enough to be still too young to get drafted. But the images of unpopular war-time activities in Vietnam and college campuses bleeding through their parents' newly popular, color-television screens into WB living rooms adversely affected everyone. The Vietnam War encroached upon all Americans and soon hit home in WB in the most brutal way possible.

Vinny Russo, a young man living down the block from Angie, had just turned 18 when his activated draft number called him to the conflict. Russo, a recent graduate of high school, had looked forward to working in his father's construction business.

Hearing of Vinny's call up saddened the Carpellos and the other families who knew him, but Vinny's parents assured them he would only have to do one tour of duty and that he would be home by next year's Christmas season. Every night for several months, many knees hit bedside floors as the neighbors prayed for the Russo boy to return home safely.

But it was not meant to be. As the following holiday season drew near, two smartly uniformed U.S. Army notification officers pressed the Russo family home's front doorbell and solemnly waited. The boys' parents presented themselves at their open door, and the personnel asked for permission to step inside. In the Russo's parlor, they delivered the terrible news that their son Vinny had died in action, and his body would be coming home soon.

Gossip lines burned long and deep as the devastating news traveled fast along the block and beyond that night. Everyone living on the block on Conselyea, and other families, friends, and acquaintances who knew the young man, went outside and stood vigil on the sidewalk in front of the Russo household, spilling over into the street. Transfixed, saddened, and silent, they languished there and on the stoop, not knowing what more they could say or do, hoping their presence gave the Russo family some comfort.

After the Russo's buried their son and received Vinny's Bronze Star with Valor medal—awarded for bravery shown during combat action, that red and blue ribbon hung in their boy's honor and memory for a long time on the family's front door.

Sadness afflicted Angie every day that she saw the ribbon as she passed their home on her way to and from school. Though Vinny had been years older, she knew him as one of those guys to whom she always replied, "Hello!" from the stoop to his cheerful, "Hello!" whenever he passed her way.

Given the experiences they had encountered, a personal level of confusion about who they were and what needs and wants they had pushed its way into the teenaged worlds of Angie and her friends. Pubescent hormones and physical changes sparked acute gender awareness for Angie and her cohorts, forcing them to learn from each other how to cope with inner awakenings and inevitable transitions. Hoping to make sense of the mash-up between these pressing survival urges and the visceral images broadcast into their homes by the nightly news shows, they had no choice but to keep living and growing up to adulthood.

Despite the tumultuous times, matters went well for Angie and her small circle of close friends, soon-to-be high-school freshmen. For Angie, Dante, her best girlfriends, Gaia and Francesca, and their boyfriends, all older now, playing street games started to take a backseat to hang-outs in Dante's basement. Playing card games, conducting "serious" séances, laughing, chatting endlessly, and learning how to make out, they began to transition from girls to women and boys to men. The changes did not come easy for them, but—they did not know this at the time—neither was it ever for any generation before them!

Still, they and their parents never expected a war waged halfway around the world to affect their beloved WB. Perhaps unavoidably, both generations sat together on the stoops the way others before them had, waiting for their inevitable evolutions.

Balancing what they could do something about and what they could not control, Angie's circle of friends came to grips with growing up. No matter the killing fields of Vietnam, protests on American college campuses, high schools, and streets, WB remained a mostly peaceful state of mind for those who lived among its highs and lows, including the ever-present mayhem of the Mafia.

CHAPTER 12: FATSO'S DEBACLE

Several times a month, Freddie Ferrara, a burly, overly obese Mafioso often referred to as "Fatso" by Angie's block neighbors and others, dined in Chichi's with his British-born wife, Eliza. Tonight, watched by Wei from above the laundry, he parked in the restaurant's reserved lot.

As usual, Fatso, dressed in a signature brown and black patterned jack shirt over dark silk pants, was yelling at his wife as they walked to the restaurant. Suddenly, he smacked her across her face, escalating the din of their argument loud enough for others to make out the couple's words from as far as a block away. Already cringe-worthy, the Saturday-night incident was about to get worse.

Unable to do much else because of attention fixated on the loud, obnoxious man, horrified onlookers watched Fatso turn and swiftly *punch* his wife in the face, knocking her out cold! She dropped like a paper doll, unconscious.

Fatso turned, picked her nearly lifeless body up with the help of one of the Chichi brothers, and entered the eatery, stopping only to say, “Leave her in the coat closet to revive herself!”

Seeing the atrocity unfold before her eyes upset Angie terribly. Adding to her distress, from every stoop, she heard complaints from other people who, having just witnessed the same event, remarked how horrible they felt that Fatso went too far this time. Inexplicably, their initial reactions of shock also brought out admissions that what they just saw was not so unusual. The neighbors were sure that this was not the first time Fatso had knocked out his wife. Knowing they could not easily confront the real evil in front of them, they adjusted to what just happened with a groundswell of verbal justifications. Words overheard from other stoops, unbelievable to Angie’s ears, projected that her neighbors expected this kind of offbeat behavior!

Reason did not apply here. Apathetic shoulders shrugged, eyes looked away, people got up and left the stoops to retreat inside their homes as if nothing happened. From others, choice words erupted and spewed anger into the cool night air, yet no one thought enough to lift a single finger to help or at least report the incident! Perhaps shocked, maybe inured to any violence or too weak and confused to respond in any manner, people reacted.

Angie's emotional numbness had accumulated over a relatively small number of years, puncturing her mind and heart, and now burst, falling flat like a pin-pricked balloon. A scream of panic coursed through her body inside and reminded her of every gruesome event she had ever witnessed. The mental images drove her thoughts to the brink of madness, and she screamed, thinking, *This neighborhood breeds a lot of hate, and I don't like it! Why do people have to be so mean? And because Fatso is connected, no one in this neighborhood does a damn thing about helping Eliza? Are they too worried about getting hurt themselves?*

Watching everything unfold from above the laundry, Wei, fixated and rigid, looked at the reactions of the people watching from their stoops on the next block, including Angie; their fear and anxiety revealed how helpless they were to do anything.

The people's reactions reminded Wei of that overcast day when he stood shivering in a rice field in mainland China and saw a communist soldier shove a rifle butt into his mother's face. He had learned from his stoic, intelligent, kind-hearted parents never to show emotion to an enemy. Because of their lesson, he understood that her body shook not from fear, degradation, or cold but from her bravest attempt to defiantly stand up to the suppression she and her husband faced that day, certain that they would die—her purpose was to not show any emotion, especially toward her only child standing nearby.

The boy knew that his mother would endure whatever was coming, no matter how harsh. He understood that she would never let on to her oppressor that he was her son, knowing that by giving his identity away, she would sign his death warrant. Her enemy would kill him before them and directly in front of them for the ultimate disgrace.

Instead, Wengchan's mother held her ground even as her warm blood gushed from her mouth and threatened to weaken her physical resolve. Her vows to protect him from her death remained intact and did not undo the tapestry that was her timeless, endless love for her family.

The end, she knew, was near. Deeming the couple useless to the Motherland, the same military insurgent who busted her jaw gunned down the bleeding woman first before taking down her grief-stricken husband. The last Wengchan saw of his parents was their nearly lifeless bodies inching closer, eyes open wide and staring at him as they fell from their knees upon each other and perished.

His parents' honor and integrity were intact as their virtues seared Wei's veins anew in the moments right after Fatso's atrocity. His fists clenched at his sides now. With Fatso's helpless wife slumping to the pavement, vengeful feelings stirred within him, and he vowed retribution against the fat man, regardless of any danger or harm such a move might bring to him. Recalling his parents' silence, he knew that he would doubtless avenge Fatso's senseless act, somehow and someday.

Seeing the angst in Angie's face and body language, he only knew that he wanted to protect her the way his parents rescued him. Seeing her reaction was similar to his, Wei considered that he might have found a perfect purpose not only to help him right this despicable wrong but also find relief from the guilt of not being able to prevent his parents' last day on Earth. To protect her, he knew, would take extreme patience and gaining her attention and her trust. Resolved to tolerate whatever time that would take, Wei would wait for the right moment. He decided to protect Angie from this day forward.

Stepping back from the window and slowly closing the lacy curtain, Wei felt better. The initial framework for accomplishing the goal of rubbing out Fatso boosted his confidence, and, with that, he embraced his new self-given responsibility to protect Angie. The more he studied her and learned about her, the more she seemed to him, one who shared a natural capacity for empathy toward less fortunate people.

For now, though, Wei did not know what only Detective Scarpelli did: that a well-deserved punishment would be meted out sooner or later against Fatso for committing undetected code transgressions and high crimes against his fellow Mafiosi.

Like any common criminal, no matter how bright or high his IQ, Fatso believed that no one would ever discover his hidden activities. However, because one particular person other than Freddie "Fatso" Ferraro knew about his illegal iceberg, his remaining days on Earth numbered few. And Wei's wish would certainly come true.

CHAPTER 13: THE BIG REVEAL

"Boss, remember that kitchen fire in Chichi's?" asked Detective Scarpelli.

Molinari nodded in a way that encouraged his "employee" to continue.

"Well, I did a bit of investigating..." he hesitated and then added, "... And you're not going to like what I think I've discovered once I put the pieces of the puzzle together. And I'm going to need your help to confirm my suspicion."

Molinari turned serious and leaned in toward Scarpelli, keenly interested in what he had to say.

"I believe that for a long time, one of your soldiers has been skimming your take before he delivers it to you."

"What?! Who is it?!"

Molinari's mind simmered and, in a nano-second, moved closer to a full boil. He did not utter one word, only stared expectantly at his informant.

"Fatso!"

Molinari laughed out loud right in Scarpelli's face.

Joey Gap unexpectedly entered Molinari's office and wondered what was happening.

Surprised to see him, Molinari stood up and greeted Gap with open arms, owing to his debt of gratitude for his help to rise through the ranks to the position he now held.

Taking advantage of the moment, Scarpelli also stood up and shook Gap's hand, boasting, "Gentlemen, this is good news that you're both here!"

Scarpelli was about to relay his news to Gap, but Molinari cut him off, saying, "Get this, Joey! Scarpelli here thinks Fatso's skimming the books!"

Hearing this, Gap first looked shocked and surprised, but then he saw Molinari was about to burst out laughing again, causing both men to laugh aloud.

Settled down, in unison, they asked Scarpelli, "What are you talking about?!"

"I'm telling you the betting numbers are off, and your take isn't and hasn't been right for a long time, adding up in Fatso's territory.

"Fatso? *Really*, Scarpelli?!"

"Yes. Freddie Fatso Ferraro..." Scarpelli let it sink in and then added, "... he's been doing in you guys *for years."*

Gap reacted first, "I don't believe you! I've known Freddie for a long time! I attended every one of his weddings! Our families go back to the Old Country!"

Scarpelli repeated, "It's Fatso. Why would I lie to you?"

Molinari studied Scarpelli's face for a tell, but there was none.

"Let us see what you got!" they demanded in unison, "... Where's the proof?"

Seeing Molinari pour a Cutty shot and offer it to him, Scarpelli told his story.

"It started with the fire in Chichi's last month. I was the primary detective on the scene. Walking around the kitchen area after the firemen put out the flames, I saw wet and half-burned pieces of torn-up numbers sheets on the floor. I picked them up and stuffed them into my pockets so no one else would find them."

Molinari and Gap listened intently, quietly fuming under their skin as the story unfolded.

"... Later on, I took the papers out of my pocket and noticed on one of them the initials "FF" and on a couple of others, five or six bets placed on the numbers with parts of two names, one of which I recognized. It seemed Fatso used nicknames on the books he kept. Gentlemen, it would have been bad for all of us if some other cop saw this evidence before I did!"

Mole and Gap looked at each other with a bit more serious attitude this time—they knew that Fatso did use nicknames—and again back at Scarpelli, who continued.

"... So, as soon as I could, I burned the papers and promptly forgot about them. A couple of weeks later—I was having a drink at Chichi's, and one of the guys whose partial nickname, Bacigalupo, was on one of the sheets sat next to me at the bar. We started talking."

"Who is this Bacigalupo?" Gap asked, looking back and forth at Molinari and Scarpelli. "... Do I know him?"

"Johnny DeAngelo," Scarpelli answered. Feeling vindicated and seeing by their reactions that both men knew that name, he went on with more of his account.

"So, we were talking, and he told me he was going to take his family out to dinner with money he won at the horse track. And I said, 'I'm happy for you, enjoy!'"

Molinari motioned with his hands that Scarpelli should speed things up.

"... So, after he left, one of my other cop friends came over and told me that he won by playing the numbers on the street, not at the track. He didn't want to tell me because, you know, I'm a cop, too! We both laughed about it, and..."

"Wait a minute. Who is this cop? What's his name?" asked Molinari.

"Richie Caputo."

“Should we worry about him,” asked Gap, looking at Molinari.

“No, not at all. I believe that Richie plays numbers every week. Which bookie? I don’t know,” answered Molinari.

“Go on, finish your story,” Molinari commanded after looking at Scarpelli. The two men, not saying a word, passed a lot between them with glances toward each other.

“Caputo went on to tell me, jokingly, ‘Johnny bets at least ten bucks a day, so he must have won big money.’ It didn’t dawn on me at the time, but driving home, I remembered that next to Bacigalupo’s name on the paper, it said eight dollars, not ten. I thought Richie was mistaken...”

The boss and the capo leaned forward, anxious to hear more.

“... A week later, I saw Johnny again at Chichi’s. He came over to me and whispered in my ear that he was told by Richie that I was an okay guy and that he, too, won playing the numbers off-track. He went on to tell me that he bet ‘ten bucks every day and one finally paid off.’

But I remembered the papers, and, sure enough, his bet showed up as eight dollars, not ten."

Warmed up, Scarpelli brought out more details.

"*That's funny,* I thought. *Richie was not mistaken.* I then recalled that another partial name on another paper included the word 'Meat' and that this person bet three dollars daily. I started asking around who has the nickname 'Meat,' and it turned out there was some guy nicknamed, 'Meatball!'"

Molinari encouraged Scarpelli with another round of Cutty, which the detective tossed back.

"I was thinking *I gotta get a hold of this guy*. So, I went to Chichi's, hoping I would bump into Bacigalupo—Johnny, I mean—and, after several nights of sitting at the bar and tumbling the cubes in my Cutty, he was nowhere around...."

Gap cuts in, "You gonna get to the point anytime soon?"

Scarpelli reacted nervously, snickered a bit, and continued.

"... The next week, as I parked my car on Conselyea, Johnny was talking to someone outside in front of Chichi's, and I said hello and asked him to have a drink with me, which he did after finishing his conversation..."

By now, Molinari and Gap were all ears.

"... I asked him if he knew someone called, 'Meatball,' and he said, 'Yeah, sure I do. Who's asking?' He told me that it's a nickname not many people know about. His name is Robert Torre, and his nickname is 'Meatball'!

"So, Johnny asked me if I was looking for the guy because he was in some kind of trouble, and I said, 'No, nothing like that.'"

" 'Then why are you interested in him?' he asked.

" I told Johnny that I had heard from Richie that he might be my *paesano*, something about his father and my father coming from the same town in Italy.

"In other words, I lied.

"... Using Richie's name as the source of our conversation was fine because he goes along with me on anything.

"'Oh,' Johnny said, 'I'll introduce you to him!' So, we made plans to meet at Chichi's the following week.

"... At the bar, the three of us sat and talked about our families and found that we had no common relationship. Our fathers didn't even come from the same town. All of which, of course, I knew.

".... So, we were sipping drinks, and I said that it's great news about Johnny winning big on his bet, and they reacted. At first, Torre (Meatball) looked at Johnny, and Johnny gave him a nod that it was okay, that I could know.

"So, he told me, 'Yes' and that he wished he could win big like Johnny someday, too, but that if he does ever win, it wouldn't be much because he 'only bets five dollars per day, not like Johnny's ten-dollar bet....'"

Molinari and Gap look at each other, lightbulbs switching on in their heads simultaneously.

"... And then, it all came together: Johnny betting ten and only eight appeared on the sheet; Robert betting five and only three dollars marked the sheet. The more I remembered the bits of paper with 'FF' on them; they were all like that!"

"Fucking, son-of-a-bitch," Gap exclaimed, 'This is very hard for me to believe!" He told Molinari to investigate this to the fullest extent immediately.

Molinari to Scarpelli, "I hope you're wrong about all this."

"I know how you both feel about Fatso, and I wouldn't have brought this news to you, Victor, if I didn't think it was true. Joey, I'm just sorry that you had to hear this from me."

Molinari directed Scarpelli with Gap's approval, "Keep your nose to the ground, Scarpelli, and make sure I know as soon as you know whatever additional information you find on this."

"Loud and clear, boss!"

By the time Scarpelli left the Social Club by way of the back alley, Molinari and Gap had already picked up their phones and were dialing familiar numbers. As Gap departed, they agreed to meet again if and when they had corroborating information to share to protect their flanks.

From Molinari's watch in Manhattan, the latest reports that came in from trusted soldiers showed extremely damning evidence against Fatso. He had been skimming the operation's numbers take for more than a decade! Enraged, Victor called Gap, who went ballistic on hearing the report. He fired back, "I'll be right over! We need to talk!"

Molinari had already poured two shots of Cutty and had put them on his desk by the time Gap breezed in, shouting obscenities. He tried to play it cool to counter Gap's high-decibel mood, but his words took on a life of their own, further stoking Gap's fire, "I can't believe this fucking Fatso! For years, right under my fucking nose! I had my guys dig deeper. We analyzed ledgers going back 10-12 years. There's more than four hundred grand gone missing!"

Gap reacted, "Are you fucking kidding me?!"

"I wish I were. We questioned over 50 people who've played numbers with Fatso for years, and the situation is just as Scarpelli told us."

"How does it go?" asked Gap.

"Say, a player gives Fatso ten dollars... he writes it down as $8.00, takes two for himself right off the top. He would then make eight-dollar bets, not ten."

"What if someone won?"

"He paid the full winning amount, the fucking scumbag! How often does that happen? He robbed us blind! He screwed us bad, Joey. And for a long time!"

"I've heard enough. You know what you have to do. You have my blessing."

"I fucking want him *gone,* Joey."

"Do it, but use someone you fucking trust a hundred percent."

Gap finished his Cutty and stormed out of the room. The last sound he heard was Victor on the phone, asking Wei to meet him in person, "Tomorrow, 'cause I got important work for you!"

Not knowing it, Fatso now walked and breathed with a target squarely painted on his body now. The coming contract by the end of the day would be only a matter of where and when.

CHAPTER 14: WEI GETS HIS WISH

Molinari never shared information with his cleaners beyond the price and a target contract photo under usual circumstances. This hit targeted someone within their ranks, so he told Wei about the scheme that Fatso waged against him, Gap, and the organization, adding, "I'm telling you all this because you need to know this job comes from the Boss himself, Joey Gap. We need this done as soon and as discreetly as possible, no loose ends, *capische?*!"

"Understood!" answered Wei, as usual, a man of few words and as much action as required to get his work completed.

"In a few days, you will hear from me with further instructions on where and when we want this done, and you will fulfill this contract for us with no questions asked."

Wei nodded, despite Molinari's apparent disregard of his right to choose details for a hit. While he never considered any hit he performed to be personal, just pure business, this time, it was different for him because he *wanted* Fatso dead. His emotions had blurred the moment he witnessed Fatso punch his wife. From that time, like black mold, his childhood past had crept back into his adult mind and relentlessly reminded him of his parents' senseless slaughter. Upset, he was not aware of how much those thoughts controlled and affected him now. Motivated by what he had just learned, he itched to help Fatso take his last breath as soon as possible. For him, this sanction stretched well beyond the contract's terms. Now that he had official permission to satisfy his craving, his mind and heartbeat quickened to take on the crusade.

The outcome of Wei's meeting with Molinari could not have been better. Yet, as anxious as he felt, the assigned task's execution would have to wait for a call from Molinari. Or so he thought until Molinari called him at home, surprising him with one more enticing tidbit to chew on, "Wei, Joey Gap just called, and you have carte blanche. Get it done quickly!"

CHAPTER 15: STOOPBALL & MAYHEM

"Yo, 'Stoop Girls!' We're gonna beat you so bad!" yelled the teenaged boy who, with unabashed bravado, strutted and high-stepped his legs and flapped his folded arms like a rooster on parade before hens.

Angie, JJ, Francesca, Anna Maria, and Gaia had never thought about giving themselves a team nickname. On this cloudless, humid summer afternoon, they felt no differently about that as they readied themselves for a fierce game of stoop ball off Angie's stoop against a ragtag, hastily assembled team of boys from the neighborhood.

Angie, the girls' captain, parried the provocative challenge, "Yeah, well, you might think so, but you're gonna have to get a better ball! This one's got no bounce!"

It was true, too. She turned and threw what should have been a perfect pointer—so named because the ball hits the top edge of one stoop step, and the result is a ball that earns home-run points by sailing across the entire street too fast and too high to be caught on the fly or after only one bounce—and it fell flat.

"This isn't even a 'Spaldeen,'" she rubbed in perfect "Brooklynese," once the ball was back in her hand.

Embarrassed, the boys reluctantly agreed they needed a better ball. Both girls and boys dug into their pockets for spare change. With enough gathered to satisfy their need, several members of both teams walked the few blocks to Mary's Candy Store and purchased a half-dozen Spaldings for twenty cents apiece, a small price to pay for a better bounce. They bought the lot because Conselyea Street sloped downward, and players lost more balls than could be retrieved from under parked cars before the sewers at the block's end swallowed them whole.

Brisk play ensued. To the chagrin of the other team, the girls won. The score, 100 points to 10, forced the losers to slink home with their tails between their legs. From then on, the Stoop Girls sobriquet stuck like a badge of honor.

Savoring the win, the girls retired to the Carpello stoop to cool off, relax, and see who or what would unfold before them the rest of the afternoon. They did not have to wait long for the action to appear.

Having stepped away from the LL-train subway exit stairwell on Metropolitan Avenue and walked toward where Union Avenue intersected Conselyea, barely noticed at first, Peter Wei stepped off the curb and crossed the street. He walked on Conselyea toward the girls. Overdressed in a three-piece, pinstriped suit, gripping a weather-beaten leather valise in one hand, he managed a barely visible wave with his other upon nearing the Stoop Girls.

Seeing Wei so dressed up on a warm day prompted JJ to ask, “Mister, what’s with the suit?”

Addressed directly, he stopped, surprised. He turned and answered JJ, “My day off. I feel happy.”

Gaia asked, “Why so happy?”

“Payday!”

"We've seen you before... do you work in the Chinese laundry?" asked Francesca.

"I work laundry, yes." He pointed to the laundry on the next block.

Wei's eyes surveyed the girls, and he crisply commented on how he always sees so many people sitting outside on the steps in front of their houses. He watched to see if Angie would react, too.

"Pardon me; I always wonder *what are those steps?"*

JJ instantly chimed in, "Everybody enjoys the stoops after winning a game, which we just did, or after a meal, but sometimes just because it's a nice day outside."

"Aah, I see." Puzzled, he asked, "'Stoop?" in a manner not overtly revealing his budding impatience at what he thought was obvious reluctance from Angie to engage with him.

"The stoop is this place, these steps. You know, where we hang out," JJ clarified.

The girls said nothing more. None had ever before spoken to this odd man, although they had seen him and watched from the warm familiarity of the stoop whenever he went by on his way to the laundry on the next block.

The dandy bowed slightly at the waist and thanked JJ for her knowledge and kindness. Smiling at the girls and shooting a furtive glance toward Angie, which she saw, he continued his walk toward Lorimer, apparently satisfied with what he had learned.

Once their visitor put several yards between them and was out of earshot, Anna Maria half-whispered, "Oh, man! Can you believe it? That guy didn't even know what a *stoop* is!"

Francesca hissed, "Can you imagine?"

"Ditto!" said JJ in her usual enthusiastic style.

"For sure, gotta be from some other planet, not from WB," concluded Gaia, accepting nods of approval from the other girls, every one of them giggling, except Angie, who had more to say.

"... Look at us, the Stoop Girls... we know what a friggin' stoop is! How incredible that he didn't. Sheesh!"

"You got that right," chimed Francesca.

Angie then cited what stoops meant to her.

"I should have told him this: a stoop, if you must know, is a flight of stairs attached to the outside of row houses and brownstones. You walk up a stoop of stairs, approach the front door, ring the bell or knock on the door, and you say 'Hello!' And, sometimes, you have to tiptoe around people sitting on the stoop."

The Stoop Girls' heads nodded with an enthused agreement as JJ, smacking and popping her gum, added:

"As a word, stoop comes from Old English stūpian, a verb of Germanic origin dated from the late 16th century. Stoop, "a small porch," derives from the

Dutch stoep pronounced the same as stŏŏp. Anyway, to us, my friends and family, this is our hang-out spot!"

"Whoa, Sis! I never read about that! I'm impressed!" exclaimed Angie.

JJ's girlfriends showered her with an appreciative round of applause, to which she stood up and performed a mock curtsy accompanied by a loud POP! from her wad of Dubble Bubble.

Suddenly, a car horn blasted from the end of the block. Angie and her friends swiveled fast enough to see the eccentric Chinese man deftly sidestep a car that almost knocked him down, its driver waving his arm and a middle-finger salute from his open drivers-side window. Without missing a beat or dropping the valise now tightly clutched to his chest, Wei skipped safely across Conselyea and Lorimer and disappeared into the Chinese laundry.

A water main break had closed the business for a couple of weeks, which fit perfectly into Wei's real plans. The laundry manager opened his front door upon seeing him.

He handed Wei his paycheck, commented on his sharp outfit, and inquired about his plans.

"Business, meet someone from Taiwan," he lied.

The manager, also on Molinari's payroll, only knew that Wei ran numbers and occasionally operated a press in his shop.

"Must pay plumber. Here is key. You lock up, okay?"

"No problem."

Wei took the key. He watched the manager go outside, get in his car, and drive away before he headed to the backroom and his secure locker there. Opening it and surveying his options, he selected a weapon, changed into less formal attire, and slipped out a side door to where he thought prying eyes would not see him.

The consummate professional, Wei took seriously any contract. With one hand gripping his silenced weapon at the back of his belt under his loose shirt, he was ready to take out his intended target anytime, anywhere.

CHAPTER 16: THE DAYLIGHT HIT

A man shouted something in Italian, a loud POP! POP! shattered the air, and two barely audible "PFFT-PFFTs" followed, startling Angie and her friends. They turned, seeing nothing unusual, but the harshest reality of the WB environment had already rushed into their minds: someone possibly had just shot someone!

Heads from every occupied stoop on the block turned in the direction of the gunshot-like sounds. Now people expected to see what—they did not know—would come from around that corner.

No more than a handful of anxious minutes of silent wondering passed before Wei opened the front door of the Chinese laundry, stepped out wearing the same suit he wore going in, and turned and locked the door. He clutched tightly to his chest a large laundry shirt box. Unknown to anyone else, hidden inside were his leather valise and a warm gun. Walking in the opposite direction on Conselyea and on the other side of the street from Angie's stoop, he headed toward Union at his usual unhurried pace. His fedora hung at the same tilt, and his eyes focused only forward on his intended destination, not the people he knew were watching him.

"AT LEAST, YA KNOW WHAT A STOOP IS NOW, HUH?!" yelled Angie loudly, forcing all eyes and ears on the block to fall upon her. She had failed to capture his attention, it seemed, because Wei kept moving at his usual pace, except at the split-second after her words smote the air like lightning, he briefly had touched one forefinger to the brim of his hat, perhaps a salute of sorts. He also tautened the ends of his lips upward in as brief a smile as possible—a deliberate twitch so designed that not one person would ever be able to see it. His satisfaction at accomplishing both of his mission goals, to kill Fatso, and to make contact with Angie, was intact and broadening. Wei felt a warm glow inside his chest, over which he whispered, "*Xiexie*," in gratitude to his parents as he flicked his eyes skyward for a split second.

Feeling smug, Angie turned and looked around at her friends' faces, white as ghosts. She felt pretty sure she had done the right thing, thinking, *This is our block, too,* while saying aloud, "What?!" and shrugging her shoulders.

Nobody on the block suspected that the mysterious stranger played a role in the shooting, and he was certainly not sticking around to tell anyone his business. He intended to get out of there as fast as possible, just as the first wails of police car sirens shattered the block's pregnant silence punctuated by whispered chatter here and there.

Before long, uniformed foot patrolmen from the 90th Precinct parted and controlled the growing crowd gathered at the corner.

Like the others, Angie did not know what exactly happened, and neither did her friends and neighbors.

Not one Stoop Girl or block neighbor noticed the single trickle of sweat that slid down the departing man's right temple, ever so slightly marring his facial pancake makeup. Nor did they see the powder burns on his right hand which he had rinsed with water as best he could before leaving the sanctuary of the laundry.

Watching the mysterious man's silhouette diminish with every step, none of the girls wise-crack guffawed or showed disrespect. Perhaps they were still startled from what they thought they heard, gunshots, and were wondering more about the fact that the unusual man had just today, for the first time, engaged in small talk with them. But perhaps parental admonishments and upbringing silenced their thoughts from becoming remarks that would bring trouble.

Trouble in the Italian sector, nobody wanted that! Ever-present Mob members standing by with open ears and nasty habits specialized in *taking care of* real or rumored, innocent or guilty problems! They brandished a persuasive style of getting their business done. Never crossing paths with them was desirable, even vital, to anyone's health!

Continuing on Conselyea, turning the corner, and then heading to the subway entrance on Metropolitan, all Wei thought about was boarding a train headed back to the safe anonymity of Chinatown.

For the next several hours, police foot patrolmen and armed detectives converged on Lorimer Street, encouraging anyone who might come forward to speak up about what they had heard, if not seen. But there were no takers.

Some of the detectives took to the other streets to gather more information.

"You guys on the stoop! Any of youse seen anything?"

A group of boys merely shook their heads from side to side.

Detective Scarpelli walked up to the patrolman who had asked the guys.

"You get anything? "

"Not on your life, detective. Nobody's seen anything. Strange, huh?"

Scarpelli's eyes scanned over the young guys and other clumps of people, and single individuals watching from stoops and inside the houses and shook his head.

"Officer, you're not going to get anything from these people, trust me. You might as well pack it in."

The men turned and walked back to the corner. The crowd was dissipating nearly as fast as the police cruisers left the scene.

Later, a new team of officials entered the scene and tried again to get a verbal report on the incident. These two detectives stopped and talked with the DeMarco family across the street from Angie's house. The Stoop Girls, of course, could overhear the conversation.

One undercover officer introduced himself, "Good day, I'm Detective Timothy O'Connor from the New York Police Department. My partner here is Frank Esposito. There was a shooting a little over an hour ago on Lorimer. We're investigating the incident. Did you see or hear anything?"

Mr. DeMarco answered, "No, not at all. We just came out on the stoop about five minutes ago. We were inside and didn't see or hear anything."

"Thank you, sir."

The detectives continued to canvass the block, crossing over to the other side of the street. Watching them closely, Anna Maria said to her Stoop Girl mates, “I hope they don’t come asking us any questions.”

“Well, I don’t know what that sound was anyhow. It could have been a car back-firing,” said Gaia.

Francesca suggested they get active, taking her cue: “Let’s start a game of stoop ball.”

Angie stepped down to the pavement and started the new contest with a smartly executed home-run pointer.

Before long, the detectives did approach the girls, interrupting their play.

“Hey, girls, who’s winning?”

JJ answered, “I’m the youngest, and I’m winning!”

The detectives smiled; everyone else just stared at her.

“A shooting took place on Lorimer earlier this afternoon. Did any of you see or hear anything unusual?”

The girls, silent, looked at each other blankly.

Then, Gaia said, "I think I heard a car backfire, maybe two or three times. But we didn't hear anything else. We've been playing stoop ball most of the afternoon, yelling and screaming at each other."

O'Connor and Esposito knew the girls had just started their game but thanked them anyway and walked away toward Lorimer.

"Tough neighborhood, Esposito."

"The toughest, O'Connor. In this neighborhood, people look but do not talk. And I can't blame them: they don't know who's pulling strings. The last thing these people want anything to do with is whatever might be Mob-related. The unwritten rule around here is that sealed lips help you stay out of trouble!"

"Why do they do that? Don't they realize we're only trying to help them?"

"That's how their grandparents and parents taught them to respond to situations, my friend, especially if it's a life or death situation!"

There was certainly never any shortage of drama in the WB community, just never anything much said about it.

Eventually, the charged atmosphere settled back to normal, and the departure of Angie's girlfriends left her mind free to wander around before settling upon second thoughts about the man she would someday come to know, Peter Wei.

* * *

Wei knew that from this day forward, his life changed forever. He had fired his gun twice, albeit in self-defense since the mark—Fatso! — had fired at him first in broad daylight in the most visible manner possible: on the street in the open and under broad sunlight where anyone could see them! He had not wanted the hit to go down that way and never would have planned such an event, especially at that time of day.

Wei instantly felt ambushed, but he hoped that was not the case because he would have to deal with an unknown he had not counted upon: someone inside wanting him wiped out. If that were so, he had no clue who that could be other than his employers, Molinari or Gap.

On the train, the events of the day played over and over in his head. Thinking about how he had defended himself with the silenced gun, he expressed self-doubts. *I survived but at what cost?*

Wei continued to reflect on what happened.

The shooting? Matter of seconds. I stay only to change and leave laundry; sure there would be investigation. I right about that; police appear fast, cordon off area.

He worried, too.

Was I set up? Why Fatso shoot at me? I the target, or someone else? Fatso know about me? About hit? How he know he my target if he did know? Coincidence? Maybe not!

Wei knew he could not take any chances; everything had to be buttoned down. Now that he had left the area, perhaps an extended vacation someplace else in the world made the most sense. He knew that he had no idea who caused the incident to occur the way it did—in his mind, someone had to have planned something that bizarre!

Fitfully, Wei lightly closed his eyes and tried to rest as the subway car carried him to Manhattan.

Once in his apartment, almost no longer able to keep his eyelids open, before he fell asleep, he remembered a promise to call Molinari and dialed the capo's number.

Picking up his phone on the first ring, Molinari, expecting to hear from Wei, asked only, "You okay?"

"Fine. No more fat man, I clean up."

"Good. Fatso's gone, then. Good.

"Shooting surprise me, ambush."

"I understand. So, look, get out of town for a while. Fatso was a long-time made-man, and the cops knew him. They will probably investigate, fearing a civil war. I need to clamp that down.

"Don't worry, Wei. I've worked with you, and I know this is not your M.O... you're always discreet and clean. Something else went down, is my guess, but you're not to worry about Gap or me. We know you're the best, and hey, you took out your target!"

"No one knew today was the day, not even you. You gave me carte blanche."

"I know I did, don't worry. We're cool about it. Call me when you're in a safe place. If there's another a traitor among us, we'll find them."

Relief poured off Wei after speaking to Molinari and realizing no one set him up. He thought *Molinari would get to the bottom of what happened, of that I'm sure.*

CHAPTER 17: LAYING LOW

Say what you will about the Mafia's intentions and objectives; they have their own set of rules and mores. They punish any member who breaks the rules or the status quo, anyone who draws attention to themselves and their peers by bad behavior. Fatso did all of that; it was just a matter of time before his elimination was necessary. Above his rank, the powers led him on quietly, watching which way the wind swept across his quarters before they confirmed to blow him away forever.

None of the other WB capos ever thought Fatso would go out the way he did. Molinari and Gap never told them before, not wanting to risk his getting away with a lesser sentence than death. Neither did they ever disclose their Chinese connection.

What Fatso had done to all of them deserved this kind of punishment. The other capos and a few of the soldiers kept in the loop only knew that Fatso was loyal, that he was one of them. In turn, they trusted him, making his sins gone public even more treasonous. Not a single Mafia soul ever suspected that Fatso cooked his books and skimmed from the take—a high-risk, suicidal move for anyone of any rank among their crowd!

For the moment, Molinari and Gap were trying to figure out if and how Fatso had known there was an active contract out on him. And who the shooter would be!

Wei had done the deed based on the evidence put in front of him. The two top bosses had sanctioned the hit. He even had waited for what would be the most opportune moment to make the hit in the darker recesses of Chichi's parking lot. He had surveilled the lot for weeks from above the laundry. He knew the spot that would be the perfect location if he ever had to make an inside hit, and he was aware of the days Fatso visited Chichi's.

Yet, something went awry. A hit in broad daylight out on a street where who knows who could witness the whole event was intolerable!

And so, relieved of duties and feeling certain that Molinari would get to the bottom of the situation, Wei chose his destination, a place no one would ever expect him to go or be: the island nation of New Zealand, far away in the South Pacific. He figured, once there, he would blend in among the significant and growing Chinese immigrant population.

Having heard of the tremendous concentration required by the sport and the large numbers of fish, trophy-worthy lunkers included, lying in the Kiwi rivers and streams, he thought he might try his hand at fly fishing. The added benefit that he would be in remote areas far from cities or towns. Being accompanied only by hand-chosen, licensed fishing guides who would never press him for details of his "other" life appealed to him. To them, a willing foreigner with wads of cash and a desire to fly-fish was sufficient drama and enough reason to take him on as a client.

Upon his arrival at Auckland and after an excursion to a smaller harbor town a couple of hours away by car, he phoned Molinari and let him know where he was.

Once he heard Molinari's voice, he only said, "Waihi."

"Good choice. Good fishing nearby. Gold mining, too," was all Molinari said.

"So I hear."

Wei hung up the phone. His attention was already far away from the daily routines of WB and, for the time being, even Angie!

CHAPTER 18: LETTING GO & FACING REALITY

Come September, Angie enrolled in her first high school classes with her friend Gaia Carnivale. Because the local neighborhood public high school was no longer safe to attend due to racial tensions, they took classes at St. Agnes High School, a multi-racial, all-girls school in WB, a 20-minute bus ride away.

Although Angie added lots of friends to her roster, she and Gaia continued to hang out with each other. Both loved going to this high school, and they performed better academically because of the emotional support they received from the new friends they made. Outside of the classrooms, they continued to explore their deepest feelings about love, boys, and the loyalties they felt toward each other.

Angie did not have one clique that she belonged to, but several. With Gaia and an additional five friends, Mary, Rosie, Samantha, Kelly, and Bella, a group they dubbed the "Magnificent Seven" lunched together every day. The grouping brought together several nationalities, and the Italians always had the best lunches. Caterina prepared fresh lunches for Angie every weekday, whose favorites were Chicken Cutlet Milanese with lettuce on a roll, Genoa salami on Italian bread, or a sandwich made with tuna fish in olive oil smothered with mayo and onions. Always fresh and *delizioso*!

Knowing that Angie's friend, Mary, loved her tuna fish sandwiches, Caterina always made an extra for Mary when making one for Angie. And when Rosie's mom passed, she made an extra sandwich of genoa salami, Rosie's favorite.

Toward the end of their freshman year, the Magnificent Seven accompanied other classmates and several nuns on a Catholic retreat to Shelter Island. While their idea was to have a lot of fun hanging out together for the weekend, the nuns had another purpose in mind: to moderate "rap-sessions" designed to help the girls understand themselves and each other better and get closer to God.

Nearly every attendee disliked the arranged sessions and looked forward to their free time, which was "freedom-of-choice" time to them, albeit with highs and lows.

One night, while most girls sat on the beach and talked, several decided to smoke pot. None of the girls understood how serious the situation could get until a few girls got too stoned and needed chaperoning by some others all night.

That whole summer following the Shelter Island retreat weekend, the attendees thought that the pot-smoking escapade had gone unnoticed and that they were in the clear when they returned to school in September.

Not necessarily so!

Once back on their home turf, the nuns conducted more rap sessions in a veiled attempt to unearth what happened that night! They singled out Angie and pressed her to tell them what happened on the sandy beach and who perpetrated the events. Rather than open her up more, the nuns' crusade only served to make Angie clam up along with the classmates who had attended the retreat and held to a tacit understanding every bit as strong as the general

WB neighborhood; no one ratted on their friends! Once a week for quite a few weeks, the Magnificent Seven participated in the rap-session inquisition run by the nuns, yet not one snitched on another.

The nuns gradually gave up their search, and the girls who had gone on the retreat never again trusted them.

Angie enjoyed her time in high school. When she and her new best friend Valentina got together, they shared stories of their days at school. Valentina loved to hear Angie's high-school experiences because she was looking forward to high school the following year.

One such story included the day that Bella brought a bottle of Southern Comfort to school. She hid it in the home-room closet—it happened to be in the same room as her history class—and then brought it out in the classroom just before the history teacher, Mrs. Aquino, entered. Holding the bottle up for all the other students to see it, including Angie and Gaia, Bella slugged down some of the Southern Comfort, inadvertently dropping the nearly full bottle, spilling liquor and glass shards all over the floor, stinking up the whole room!

Mrs. Aquino, of course, on her entrance, smelled the liquor and demanded to know who brought the bottle to school. No one in the class said a word, staying loyal to each other. The whole class ended up in dreaded detention after class for an hour!

Mrs. Aquino liked to dress fashionably, and, on occasion, she tucked her long black hair under a stylish, short wig. Bella, remembering that the whole class had to endure detention, decided to act. Within a week, when Mrs. Aquino had her back to the class, writing on the blackboard, Bella spit her chewing gum onto her fingers and then threw it at the teacher's head, landing the sticky wad in her wig.

Startled by the sudden commotion from the students behind her, Aquino turned and asked, "What just happened?" Then she touched the back of her head.

The students in the classroom were fit to be tied, laughing uncontrollably.

Mrs. Aquino said nothing beyond her question until the following day when she demanded to know who threw gum into her wig.

"Tell me now," Aquino said, hands on her hips. She repeated herself several times, each time clapping her hands in futile attempts to command attention.

Of course, no one ratted on Bella, so the whole class got another hour of detention! Loyal to a fault, the class endured two unwanted after-hours sessions because of Bella's prank, yet not one student ever gave her up. They were following the prevailing attitude of *let's not get anyone else in trouble.* To the students, the relationship with Aquino was an "us" versus "them" scenario.

"Wow!" cried Valentina, "... Who is this Bella?"

"Oh, I have to let you meet her so you can see for yourself. Believe it or not, Bella is as smart as a whip when she's not stoned."

* * *

Angie's growth toward her womanhood included facing up to sadnesses that involved her all-girls-high-school mates.

Kathy Murphy sat behind Angie in sophomore homeroom, the daily period lasting from 8:20 am to the bell for classes at 8:35 am. While they did not share any classes, the two girls exchanged pleasantries with each other during the few minutes they spent together before classes and, later, at the end of each school day. They liked each other and sometimes lent each other pens for the day's use in class.

One morning, while sitting in homeroom and waiting for the bell to ring, Angie noticed that Kathy was crying. Asking what the matter was, her new friend replied, "Nothing."

Over the next several days, Kathy continued to appear depressed and would only exchange small talk. A couple of weeks passed, and she went absent from school. Another week had passed when the homeroom teacher, Mrs. Ray, informed the students that she had died, without saying how.

Kathy's best friend and another classmate told Angie that Kathy had gotten pregnant, was devastated about it, and overdosed on pills and died.

Distraught and in shock, Angie remembered how she had felt close to Kathy. Upset more than her other classmates, she did not understand why the girl had gone out this way. Angie had witnessed horrendous things, but this was the first time that someone she talked with almost every day committed suicide. This act made her think that she should have pressured Kathy about what bothered her and made her sad. She had noticed something was off but never pressed Kathy about her crying; now, she thought that she might have been able to prevent the girl's senseless death and had regrets about her omission.

At home that day, she confided her feelings and thoughts to her mom, who first consoled her daughter before telling her how hard it was in her time for young girls who became pregnant.

"After all," she explained, "... like yourself today, we all were no more than children ourselves."

"But why Mom? Why did Kathy kill herself?"

"Possibly, she felt shamed; maybe she thought that she made a mistake and committed a mortal sin."

Angie listened attentively.

"... She would not be allowed to return to Catholic school because of the Church's teachings and rulings on the subject. If her parents are devout Catholics, maybe they shunned her. And it is *against the law* to get an abortion."

Caterina told Angie about teenaged friends in her time who got pregnant and endured back-alley abortions when they did not commit suicide. Many of them today had ovarian cancer from undergoing unsafe and unregulated procedures.

Angie showed signs of deep concern, so Caterina told her more.

"Unfortunately, getting a safe abortion even today requires not only knowing a doctor who agrees to perform it but also having enough money to pay for it."

Angie, horrified and scared, started to cry, and her mom consoled her with a sympathizing hug meant to quell her daughter's sadness over her lost classmate. She also mentioned that Kathy's parents should have protected her, which lightened Angie's outlook a bit. She did look a little better, but she had not fully recovered, so Caterina told her more.

"Honey, I also knew families that welcomed the birth of their child's child. Some even raised the infant as if they were their child, permitting their daughters to continue schooling through graduation."

Angie wiped dry the remains of her tears, saying, "Thanks, mom. I feel better now."

"Good, Angie, because we all have to go on living. We're all different. We have our paths to follow, don't we?"

She smiled at her daughter, and they hugged again, Caterina telling her, "C'mon, I'll cook you anything you want."

"How about pizza, Mom?"

They got busy in the kitchen.

* * *

Life in WB continued to ebb and flow like the nearby shoreline tides along Long Island's beaches. Angie, the Stoop Girls, their neighbors, and, at times, passers-by continued to gather and discuss at length a variety of topics on more than one occasion, concluding each time that from the stoops on Conselyea, constant change was the norm.

Like heartbeats, the free-flowing activities of WB continued to be sights to behold. So much happened on stoops: people celebrated love and marriage and the losses of loved ones; they purchased eggs, fruits, and vegetables from vendors, new relationships began as old ones ended; passionate lovers oblivious to anyone watching conceived families late at night and, later, raised their infants to adulthood from there. Some of those new adults stayed in WB and sparked the next generations and their stoop experiences. Families expanded and welcomed in-laws, even as other families broke down, split up, and departed.

Angie's block and stoop were among the most admired in WB. A microcosm of all things good and bad, the location found itself the residents' pride of nearby streets and avenues, representing family expressions, the Italian community's traditions here and abroad, and friendships.

There was a losing one for every winning story on the flip side, and poverty never chose sides or genders in WB. It did specialize, at times, in lost causes, like the woman in a relationship with a Mob boss who found herself down on her luck one evening. This luckless woman burst out of Chichi's alone, angry and drunk. She managed to weave her way to her car before getting behind the wheel and driving down Conselyea, rubbing paint and metal with at least a dozen parked vehicles. The drama ended when two large made-men yanked her away from the wheel. They dragged her out of the car and packed her into another that left the scene posthaste. Her empty vehicle sat in the middle of the street, blocking traffic with the motor still running.

People watched every bit of the action from their stoops, certain that there would be severe repercussions. Yet, the following day, Angelo Cicone, owner of The Body & Fender Auto Shop on the block, found on his desk an envelope stuffed with a sizeable wad of large bills. The accompanying, anonymous note directed him to "take care of" each damaged vehicle on the block. Angelo never questioned who sent the money. Grateful, he just did the work.

In the face of these ups and downs, Angie flaunted a defiant attitude when necessary, despite the daunting atmosphere surrounding her block and neighborhood residents. She was anything but a coward, and her DNA contained within its ribbons a definite streak of bravado when she thought *enough is enough!*

CHAPTER 19: CULTURE SHOCK

Sometimes, unfathomable activities originated from home and brought themselves down on adolescent shoulders. As she grew in years, Angie made more and more decisions about what was right or wrong for her; in other words, she came to understand herself more and what she would stand for behavior-wise.

On a particular Saturday morning, Angie, JJ, and the rest of the Stoop Girls were deep into another game of stickball against the boys when Caterina called out to her daughters, "Girls, come here. We have to go to Enza's house. A few things 'fell off the truck.'"

Angie thought to herself; *I just don't get it. We're taught not to steal, and now we're going to look at and most probably buy stolen clothes. That isn't right!*

Old enough now to yell back to her mom, she did, "It's a mortal sin, Mom! I'm not going!"

"Suit yourself, Angie, but I'm going, and I'm taking your sister with me." With that,

Caterina left with JJ in tow, throwing off the number of players.

Angie lost interest in the game. Quitting, she plunked herself down on the highest stoop step, rested her chin on her hands, and almost shed a few tears. Older and wiser now, she still found it difficult to resolve the clash of her faith's teachings and the great multi-generational culture divides that existed within her WB neighborhood and her immediate family.

Most confusing, she mused. *I just don't get it!*

Later, Caterina brought home merchandise from Enza's and proudly showed Angie what she bought for her. Angie did like what she saw but again protested loudly, "Mom, it's still a mortal sin, so I'm not going to wear it."

Caterina took her reaction in stride and mollified her eldest daughter.

"C'mon, I'll take you and your sister to Jerry's Candy Store,"—the one treat Angie and JJ never turned down!

Most school days after classes, Caterina took them there, and they sat at the counter, often with Francesca and Anna Maria and their mom, Felicia.

So, they went today and once again ordered their usual: a couple of frankfurters smothered in sauerkraut and yellow mustard, topped off with an authentic New York Egg Cream.

Although Angie had a good time at the store, she was still a bit upset. Her stomach was happy, but her mood combined mental stress and emotional turmoil spilling over from her boiling cauldron of thoughts about what constituted right and wrong behaviors. And then she remembered that her friend, Valentina Stanchione, was to come by and hang out with her after dinner, which raised her spirits.

Sitting on the stoop, Angie shared the news of the confrontation she just had with her mom, but Valentina had only a sense of what Angie conveyed to her, never having even remotely experienced trafficking in stolen goods. Although Greenpoint had a Mob presence, Valentina had not grown up in the all-Italian neighborhood, nor on a block where Mobsters got in people's faces, like Angie's!

"These occurrences aggravate and confuse me. I have a hard time comprehending or justifying what goes on in this crazy neighborhood in which I live. Someday, I will live someplace else," Angie complained.

Valentina replied, "I'm sorry you're upset. There's not much I can say. Anyhow, why don't we change the subject."

"Good idea."

"By the way, what *did* your mom buy for you?"

"A sweater."

"And you liked it, you said?"

"Yes."

"Will you wear it?"

"No, I won't. It's a turtleneck anyhow, and my mom knows I hate turtleneck sweaters because they itch my neck."

"Then why does she buy them for you?"

"Who the hell knows. I can't make that one out either."

They laughed.

Valentina then filled the ensuing pregnant silence.

"I love turtleneck sweaters."

"Great, I'll give you all the ones I have that I've never worn. Help yourself to the new one mom just bought me."

"Thanks, Angie! I would love to have the turtlenecks you don't wear but will pass on the one your mom bought you today that 'fell off the truck.'"

They laughed until they almost cried.

A few minutes later, the sound of Good Humor chimes rang out, and the truck came into view, interrupting the girls' conversation. Caterina, hearing the truck bells jingling, came outside and offered to buy ice cream for the girls, later sitting with them on the stoop as they ate their favorite ice-cream bars.

Caterina's friend, Helen, stopped by to talk. Both were happy to see the other, and

Caterina asked Helen about her sister's health and well-being.

"My sister is so fuckin' lucky! Her girlfriend is *blowing* her both ways to and from Florida!"

"Oh, how nice! I hope they have a good time. Florida is nice this time of the year – not too hot!"

Helen then reported that she had gone out to lunch that day with a few of her lady friends, and when the check came at the end of the meal, she said, "We each told the waiter how we intended to pay, one of us saying, 'I am blowing her,' pointing to her friend across the table. Another said, 'I am blowing those two,' and yet another said, 'I'm blowing myself.'"

"This, of course, flabbergasted the obsequious waiter caught up in the wording, and he exclaimed, 'Well, who's gonna blow *me*?!'"

Helen and Caterina had a good laugh over that. But then Caterina realized that Angie and Valentina had no idea about what Helen was saying. She explained that when they were young, she and her friends used the term "blow" whenever someone treated someone else, paid a bill, or picked up the check. (i.e., "I will 'blow' you for a movie," meaning "I will pay your ticket for a movie.")

At first, perplexed, Angie and then Valentina caught on and ended up laughing with Caterina and Helen once they understood the word's usage!

Helen, however, was not finished. She wanted to reminisce with Caterina.

"Caterina, do you know what happened to Sister Mary Sarah *after* the Church dance that one Saturday night?"

Caterina and Helen, along with their husbands, had attended the dance. Quite a few other parishioners attended as well, along with several nuns and priests. As the evening wore on, the gathering tore a page out of a raucous Hollywood script, and everyone attending having a splendid time!

Angie already knew something about this kind of outrageous party, of course, because her student-to-student grapevine ran fast and furious with old and new news and gossip!

According to Helen, Sister Mary Sarah came to her high-school classroom on the Monday following the dance with no teeth in her mouth, wearing one shoe and one slipper.

Helen pressed on: "Sister Mary got so drunk that on her return to the convent, she went straight to the bathroom, stumbled, hurting her right foot, and threw up her false teeth! Next, she accidentally flushed them down the toilet! Of course—maybe she was still hungover or embarrassed; she never told the students what happened and somehow managed to make it through the next school day!"

Caterina's genuine shock in reaction to this news made Helen comment, "Caterina, I'm surprised you didn't know this; it was the talk of the whole neighborhood."

Bewildered, Angie and Valentina did not know whether to laugh or cry about that incident, so Angie leaned over and simply whispered another story to her friend.

"Only a few months into the eighth grade, my classmates and I had a science teacher, Mr.

Cansella, who treated us in a demeaning manner. He assigned each of us a roll-call number instead of remembering and calling on us by our real names. At the beginning of the class year, he numbered the boys in alphabetical order, 1-24, and the girls from 25-41. (Mine was 28.)"

"Are you kidding me?!"

"I swear this is true! At testing times, Cansella was so afraid his students would cheat that he handed out 3"x 3" test papers! Our class complained to the Principal, but nothing changed."

"Unbelievable!"

"Yep, but we all knew that his time was coming to an end soon. One day, a girl and boy talked to each other in class while Cansella was teaching. Enraged by this, he ran down the aisle and slapped both students! And then another boy punched Cansella in the face, bloodying his nose."

"Oh my god! What happened next?"

"Mr. Cansella got fired and never returned to the school."

"Well, at least that was good!"

"Yeah, and the rest of us moved on. We could feel that we already were growing up a little too fast."

CHAPTER 20: SOMETHING NEW

A year in the backcountry of New Zealand, from Peter Wei's point of view, meant his trip had not only succeeded in bringing him quick relief from his work-related situations but also provided him a long, pleasure-filled vacation, something he never before experienced!

Because he worked in such an exacting business fraught with life-and-death scenarios with potentially deadly consequences for him, the intense focus required for fly-fishing inspired and, when done, rested him. Strong concentration on the sport's physicality and minutiae relaxed and freed his mind from Chinatown, WB concerns, and the ever-lingering mental images of his parents and their demise, which still kept him awake most nights.

Sated from more than enough fish passed through his creel to last a lifetime after a year on the rivers and streams, Wei felt refreshed emotionally. He was ready to bring his sojourn to a close and decided to call Molinari, which he would have to do outside his hotel for security and tell him that he wanted to get back to work.

Stepping out on the street to cross over to a phone booth, Wei encountered a messenger on a moped, who unexpectedly pasted a telegram to his chest as he sped past. Seeing the sender's codename, MOLE, Wei immediately scanned the message.

His employer deemed it still too soon and unsafe for Wei to return to New York. He told him to sit tight and await further instructions. Only after determining that his return would be safe and where in the world they wanted to send him would he be permitted to leave!

Two weeks passed by the time a second, detailed message arrived at his temporary residence. The larger envelope contained travel documents to get him to his next assigned destination: Naples, Italy, specifically the district of Nola. He was to stay at the villa of Lorenzo Abatelli. Within this packet of directives was a photo of a *Gigli* being carried through Nola's streets by honored volunteers participating in the centuries-old, annual *Festival di Gigli*

(Festival of the Lilies). Directed to perform food-service activities for a *paesano* of Abatelli's at a sausage food stand midway on the festival route, Wei would wait for another directive.

Once onboard a passenger-freighter booked for him by Molinari, air flights deemed too risky, Wei had over a month of leisure ahead of him. Because he liked to read, Wei used sea time to devour many details about the upcoming festival before arriving in Italy.

Tens of thousands of local people and tourists attended the 200-year-old festival that paid homage to the Nolani's patron saint, *Paolino*. As the legend goes, in or around 410 AD, North African pirates overran Nola's residents, abducting their children into slavery. One mother sobbed for the loss of her little boy. Moved by his strong feeling of compassion for the woman, the Bishop of Nola, *Paolino*, offered himself in exchange for the boy. Accepting the offer, pirates ferried the bishop off as their prisoner. Word of his courage and self-sacrifice reached a Turkish sultan who negotiated the freedom of this holy man and the children. Overjoyed by their safe return, the townspeople greeted the freed children and bishop, carrying lilies (*Gigli*) as symbols of love and purity. The homecoming developed into a sacred, annual event. The lilies, represented today by a two-ton, flower-laden steeple made of aluminum and standing eighty-two feet in height, are carried through the streets on the shoulders of hundreds of men. Alongside this procession, a boat also carried portrays *Paolino's* safe return.

Reading more, Wei learned how Brooklyn's Nola immigrants in the 1950s, through a sponsorship with the Shrine of the Madonna Church, re-created their own Gigli Festival—a fact he tucked into the recesses of his mind.

The vessel docked at Nola's port, and Abatelli's bodyguards met Wei and drove him to the capo's villa. Abatelli welcomed Wei with open arms, kissing him on both cheeks, happy to see him and wanting to make him feel safe.

After Wei had rested from his long journey, Abatelli informed his guest that Molinari expected a phone call. On the call, Wei learned that one of the Chichi brothers happened to be walking on Lorimer Street when he shot Fatso, and he had witnessed the entire episode.

"According to him, you came out of the Chinese laundry. Fatso appeared unexpectedly and took two shots at you, missing you. You then shot back twice, using a silencer, hitting him in the chest. Is that about right?"

"It is. Should I worry about this Chichi brother?"

"No, not at all. Anthony's one of us. It seems that Fatso learned that Gap and I were on to him, knew his days were numbered and wanted to go out in a blaze of misguided glory. That fuckin' Snots loudmouthed late at night in Chichi's, while at the bar, to a few others—Fatso was there within earshot—a story about a Chinese man being on my payroll..."

Wei shuddered at the thought of that.

"... So, Fatso, seeing you right after out on the street, got spooked and shot first. Snots must've seen you at the Social Club once or twice and put two-and-two together. He knew better to keep his mouth shut—what we call 'omerta,' our code of silence"—but he messed up!"

Wei had gone silent on the other end of the line, making Molinari wonder if he had explained too much and spooked him.

"... Listen, Wei, I'll deal with Snots. You don't worry, alright? Spend time as long as you like with Lorenzo, and enjoy the delicacies at the Festival. I'll see you when you get here, whenever that is. And relax!"

With that, Molinari hung up the phone, and Wei sighed with huge relief. Until this moment, he had not been aware of how much he feared for his life since the unfortunate incident. Grateful to be alive, he decided to take Molinari's advice and stay in Italy as long as the welcome carpet was out for him.

Working at the festival for Abatelli's *paesano* Lucas, Wei cut up peppers and onions to accompany the grilling sausages. The work brought him further welcome emotional and mental respite. For a week, he watched the festivities and saw so many people enjoying themselves that he looked forward to a day off when he could walk the venue with Abatelli. For now, because he blended in doing kitchen work performed in the tent's darker back areas, he retained his anonymity and was for that reason content not to interact with other people.

A couple of days later, walking with Abatelli, a stunning illusion transfixed him. In the corner of his eyes, a blurred motion and a woman's profile seemed to be Angie! Freeze-framed in his mind for a split-second, it made him wonder, *Is that the girl who shouted at me from her stoop*?

As quickly as the mirage-like image appeared, she disappeared, vanished forever in the commotion of the roused and colorful crowd.

I must be seeing things. I gotta let this stuff go! he thought.

Looking around, Wei could not see her and let go of the thought, keeping the incident to himself. After the festival concluded, he spent more time in Abatelli's company at the villa and then booked passage to New York City.

Almost two years after he left the city seeking relief from the Fatso fiasco, Wei landed back in Chinatown and the relative safety of his loft on Pell Street and waited for Molinari to summon him to his office. When the call came, he was mentally ready and physically back in shape from maintaining his workout routines in his home gym.

After kissing cheeks in greeting, Wei shared details of his time in New Zealand, aboard the boat to Italy, the Festival of the Lilies, and the education he received at Abatelli's villa. Molinari, delighted to hear about Wei's experiences, expressed that he was glad to see him after being away so long. Despite Wei receiving another call from Molinari to stay longer, neither thought that the few months he intended to stay with Abatelli in Italy would stretch to a half-year.

Curious, Wei shifted his attention and inquired about Snots and the outcome of the investigation he assumed took place in his absence.

“We warned Snots, and he’s alive. The only reason he still breathes is that we realized he had done his share of good work for both Gap and me. But he will think twice and very carefully before he ever opens his big mouth again. I don’t think he wants a concrete lunch if you get my drift.”

Wei nodded.

“Snots didn’t know who you were that night. He was jesting in the tavern when he said that I might have a Chinese man on my payroll. There was no way he knew what Fatso surmised from his remark because what Fatso suspected he had not told anyone else. For now, Snots and I are square as long as he keeps his nose clean.”

Wei squirmed a little and grimaced at the thought of Snots still being around. Molinari, seeing this reaction, tried to appease him.

“... And just so you know, if you and Snots cross paths, he’s gonna be extra courteous to you!”

With that, Molinari extended a friendly hand, which Wei shook. Molinari next suggested a plan.

"Peter, I want you to relax a few more days before you get back into the game here. I know how much you enjoyed the Festival of the Lilies, and next week at the Shrine of the Madonna Church in Williamsburg, their annual feast begins. The owners of the Hong Wu Chinese Restaurant on Mott Street have a food stand there, and I would like you to give them a hand."

Ready to get back to work, Wei answered, "Sure, boss. I know Hong Wu people."

"Good. Have a good time and, hey, keep your eyes and ears open, *Capische*?!

Wei smiled.

Molinari smiled back, feeling smug that he had correctly sized up his man. Sliding across the table between them an envelope stuffed with cash, he nodded his head with a look on his face that Wei should accept it.

Wei took the cash envelope.

* * *

Final preparations for the annual feast were on everyone's minds, especially Caterina's cousin, Anna. Responsible for recruiting volunteers to work the Feast's Bazaar, she selected Caterina and her sister Rosa Maria every year, who were honored to do so.

Meanwhile, Wei worked food preparations inside the food stand, cutting vegetables at the back of the half-enclosed tarp and drawing minimal attention from the staff and none from the general public.

At the stand, one day after the festival opened, he peeked out of the tent's side and spotted Angie walking with a small group of friends. Doing a double-take, thinking he might be seeing another mirage, like in Nola, he thought, *maybe she was really there? Did she see me there?*

This time seeing her was for real. Looking her over and watching every move she made, Wei noticed how she had grown into a young woman. Unexpectedly, Angie turned and stared in his direction, thinking she, too, saw the same Chinese man she had met on her stoop years ago.

But the connection was more than that. While the brief encounter lasted only a mere second or two, the affinities exchanged were undeniable; something undefined had just occurred, although their awareness of each other's presence was fleeting because of circumstances.

Fate alone knew what was to come for Angie and Wei. And when, where, and how that might happen.

CHAPTER 21: ADULT ANGIE AWAKENS

Early on a bright, sunny Saturday, Angie walked to meet Valentina at her house to go shopping with her on Manhattan Avenue, Greenpoint's "Main Street." Walking the 15 or more blocks, she passed Pasquale's Pork Store, crossed under the Brooklyn-Queens Expressway, away from the noisy trucks and cars speeding along Meeker Avenue and into the quiet residential streets of Greenpoint. On Russell Street, she watched women of German descent as they scrubbed and mopped their stoop steps. She noted that Italians also cared for their property, sweeping and hosing the sidewalks in front of their houses, but this was different, which helped her appreciate how other cultures lived.

Coming to Sutton Street, a block that housed Italians, Poles, Germans, and Irish, she saw Valentina sitting on her stoop, waiting for her. High-schoolers now and a bit older, the two had a lot more to talk about, including exposure to new experiences in their lives, which they could share and compare as friends often do, so she looked forward to their time together.

Angie greeted Valentina with a quick hug, and they embarked on their outing.

Because the walk to their destination from Sutton Street to Manhattan Avenue by way of Nassau Avenue was lengthy, they were glad to have time to catch up on each other's lives. Before starting their shopping spree, Angie sensed something was on Valentina's mind. She asked, "Valentina, tell me what's going on?"

"I found out from my father that my "Uncle" Mike living with my grandmother and grandfather is actually my grandfather."

Surprised, Angie had to collect her bearings.

"My brother, sister, and I were shocked when he told that to us. He said that he was telling us the true story because we were old enough now to know the truth."

"I can understand how you felt."

"There's more. My grandmother Alice had nine children, five with her husband Marco and four with her husband's brother Mike! Only when "Uncle" Mike was dying years later after Alice and Marco were dead did he tell his four children that he was their father!"

Angie listened attentively.

"Angie, I knew you would understand because you told me about your family's disturbances."

They moved on to conjecture about Valentina's grandmother possibly having been in love with the two men and that Angie's grandmother Bianca maybe had also loved her husband and Carlo at the same time.

"How strange, huh?" said Valentina.

"I guess it's possible, but how sad for them," Angie answered.

They hugged, happy to have each other's friendship.

A bit later, the two friends saw the "Frankfurter Man" selling franks and knishes from his cart on a corner. Each decided on a frankfurter smothered with mustard and sauerkraut, a Coke, and they split a knish.

Walking on, they window-shopped their way to the Army and Navy store where they bought dungarees and new construction-style boots—the latest rage at the time.

Later, Valentina confided to Angie about her mom, Harriet, having suffered a heart attack five years earlier.

"She's fine now and back to work, but I had to take over the family reins when mom was sick."

"I'm sure that was hard on you. As I think of it, you were only twelve years old at the time; sorry you had to go through that."

"I'm just worried. If mom gets sick again, I might never get to go to college."

Angie bolstered her, "What are you crazy? With your brains, you will not only graduate college but probably earn a doctorate as well."

She also pointed out that Valentina was smart, excelled at school, and got straight A's in her classes.

"Plus, you're on the Honor Roll!"

Valentina's mood had changed, and she looked better.

"Thanks for having faith in me, Angie."

Changing the subject after they had walked some more in silence, looking in the windows as they went along, Angie announced, "I'm thinking about running for the Vice-Presidency of the Student Council. If elected, I would serve in my senior year. What do you think?"

"I say go for it. You will do a great job!"

Angie told her that she shared her thoughts with other classmates and found them supportive and that Gaia offered to serve as her campaign manager.

"Oh, with her at the helm, you will win!"

"Gaia wants to create signs and banners and hand out M&Ms, Reese's Peanut Butter Cups, and Tootsie Rolls to classmates, urging them to vote for me."

"Wow, that's going to be a blast!"

"Thanks for the vote of confidence, Valentina!"

Spotting the Peter Pan Bakery known throughout Greenpoint and in parts of Williamsburg for their great donuts, they said in unison, “Let’s get donuts to top off our day!”

Soon, remnants of their favorite choices were all over their faces: a jelly donut for Angie and a chocolate-covered cruller for Valentina.

Walking back to Valentina’s house, they confirmed that they were glad to be friends and felt comfortable telling each other anything; that somehow knowing that made the world make sense to them. Being in each other’s company brought them mutual solace, celebrated with another hug before Angie departed, and walked back home.

Angie had come a long way from being the bright-eyed toddler accompanying her mother to retail stores in WB and adjacent neighborhoods to taking on responsibilities well beyond being the team captain of the Stoop Girls. Just being herself, she naturally gravitated to roles of leadership, including the Vice-President position at school—she outlasted her opponents in the school elections and won!

A couple of weeks later, the school principal picked her to deliver the daily Public Address announcements after classes because she felt they should come from a Student Council member.

Of course, Angie was thrilled!

Classes ended at 2:20 pm, and students went to their homerooms until release time at 2:35 pm. She felt more than ready to update the student body on school issues and events and took advantage of her open-mic opportunity!

In October of Angie's senior year, the Principal shockingly notified the returning student body that St. Agnes would close forever when the school year ended, explaining that the Catholic Diocese did not have the money to support the school any longer. The students and lay teachers were upset and reacted angrily before an air of depression, like a large balloon losing air, settled upon them and the entire student body. Angie's class would graduate, but all other students would have to find another school to attend the following year.

With a few individuals' help, the depression felt among the students, lay teachers, and nuns dissipated, replaced by a fighting attitude. A buzz about doing something to keep the school open perked everyone up. The lay teachers proposed taking a pay cut, which the diocese rejected, saying the offer would not help enough to avoid the dire cost situation they faced.

At the Student Council meeting following the announcement, more than 100 teachers and students attended, including The Magnificent Seven. From that session came a decision to help keep the school open by picketing the Catholic Diocese building in downtown Brooklyn.

Collectively asking, "How are we going to go about doing this?" the Student Council realized the need for the entire student body and teachers combined to conduct a giant rally. The idea was to get everyone committed to a single date to play hooky from school classes and join the picket line. Not knowing what side the nuns would fall and assuming they would almost certainly have to back up the diocese, the students and teachers kept their plan among themselves.

Attendees of the next Student Council meeting planned how to get everyone involved. They spoke about picking a date and making flyers to inform the students and lay teachers of when the rally would happen. During this planning session, Angie proposed that before they handed out the flyers to the student body, she could, since she had access to the public mic, announce the event on the PA system and inform the student body all at once.

"The Principal never asks me in advance about what I would want to report, preferring to hand me only what she wants me to convey. The rest of an announcement would be up to me," she revealed.

In this regard, Angie predicted smooth sailing! The council then picked a day of the week for Angie to announce the picket date.

On the appointed day, Angie chose first to announce the usual daily information. When nearly finished, she added, "None of us want our school to close. The Student Council proposes that none of us come to school on November 17th; instead, report to the Catholic Diocese building at 8:30 a.m. sharp with banners and signs. We will picket to keep our school open!"

In response, thunderous applause streamed through the entire school's hallways from each classroom, which Angie could hear, boosting her confidence.

On "Picket Day," more than 500 students and teachers attended the rally, receiving a New York Daily News write-up with photos!

Unfortunately, with the school's fate sealed, it did close, but not before hundreds of hearts swelled with pride: the students and lay teachers had done their parts by trying their best to effect a change.

As interesting as her childhood was, also prepping her for adulthood by myriad WB experiences, Angie would discover more intrigue in her rapidly approaching future.

CHAPTER 22: ANGIE'S DILEMMA

One Friday night, Angie bid goodbye to her friend Diana and left her house on Metropolitan Avenue around 11:00 pm, walking her usual route home toward Leonard Street. At the corner, she turned right and headed to Conselyea. About to turn left onto her block, she heard what sounded like a couple of loud camera clicks ahead of her, and she saw a furtive man briskly walk toward the next block of Conselyea. The stranger wore dark clothing, but she could make out a few of his facial features as he passed under a street lamp.

Afraid and a bit confused, Angie retraced her steps on Leonard back to Metropolitan and from there walked toward Lorimer Street, intent on quickly getting home. Approaching her stoop and taking the steps up to the front door, she saw police cars with sirens and lights blaring speed past her, headed to the next block. The sight ignited her emotions and frightened her.

Just as she was about to put her key in the lock, her parents opened the front door.

Startled, she jumped back from the unexpected opening and saw Caterina and Luigi standing right in front of her. The three of them stepped out onto the sidewalk to watch what was going on in the next block. JJ followed soon after.

All over their block, bedroom lights lit up. Awakened residents threw on robes and slippers and stepped outside to see what was taking place. Some walked out to the middle of the street to stand and watch from there.

Police cordoned off Conselyea between Lorimer and Leonard. Among the residents, questions and gossip ran like wildfire. People stared and shook their heads, some asking passersby coming from that direction what was happening.

From a young couple who had been out for a casual walk, they heard, "There was a shooting! A man was playing cards with friends and got shot and killed. The shots were from outside the window!"

Angie overheard, and her mind raced. Her heartbeats quickened, and she thought, *Oh my god, is that what I heard?* Panic-stricken and nauseous, she kissed her parents, said a quick "Goodnight," ran into the house straight to her bedroom, and lay on her bed. Staring at the ceiling and enduring a mental hurricane, she thought,

I saw that man walking away from the houses on the next block. Did he do the shooting? Oh no, did he see me? Did someone else hear what I heard? I never saw that man before. I can still picture him in my mind. Who was he?

After what seemed to her like hours, she mercifully fell asleep, exhausted.

Simultaneously, NYPD officers canvassed the street, asking if anyone had seen or heard anything significant, but no one offered a clue. The next morning, more officers fanned out to residents on adjacent blocks and tried to piece together what happened in the shooting incident.

Detectives Vince Bolleri and John McCaffrey, assigned to talk to Leonard Street residents between Metropolitan and Conselyea, stopped first at the house of Michael and Patti Portinari. They rang the bell, and Patti answered.

Identifying themselves, they entered the couple's living room.

Bolleri began the questioning, "We're investigating a shooting that occurred last night around 11:15 pm. Did you see or hear anything?"

Patti answered, "I was getting ready for bed, and it was very quiet in that part of the house."

Michael added, "I heard a clicking sound, like a camera, but didn't think too much of it. It didn't sound like a gunshot to me, and my window was open. I had just bent over to close it. Otherwise, as my wife said, it was very quiet. I did see a teenage girl walking on the street, though. Nothing that concerned me."

Detective McCaffrey asked, "Do you know who the young girl was?"

"No."

"In which direction was she walking?"

"Toward Metropolitan."

After a few more questions, the detectives left the Portinari's and, outside, stopped to speak to an older man sitting on his stoop.

"Good Morning," Detective Bolleri said as both men showed their badges.

The older man, Sam Spinelli, shook hands with them and volunteered to them that he'd "... had two glasses of Chianti earlier, and I fell asleep before eleven."

The detectives thanked Spinelli, moved on to the next house, and rang the bell.

Leo Rossi answered his doorbell. Bolleri and McCaffrey showed their badges and asked if they might enter.

Adele Rossi walked from the dining room through the parlor and to the entrance to her home. Standing next to Leo, she invited the men to come in and sit with them at the kitchen table.

McCaffrey informed them of the shooting and asked whether they saw or heard anything.

Mr. Rossi said, "What shooting? All was quiet."

Adele backed him up, “Very quiet! But all I saw through the window was a teenage girl walking alone, who passed by our house.”

The detectives glanced at each other, and one asked, “What direction was this girl walking?”

Adele responded, “Toward Conselyea.”

Bolleri and McCaffrey looked at each other again. They had conflicting reports: Mr. Portinari saw a girl walking toward Metropolitan Avenue, and now Adele Rossi answered that a girl was walking toward Conselyea.

“Mrs. Rossi, do you know who the girl was?”

“No.”

Perplexed, the detectives left. Once outside and on the sidewalk, Bolleri commented, “Is it one girl or two?”

“I know. Portinari saw a girl going one way, and Rossi saw a girl walking the other way. At about the same time.”

“Yeah, we don’t have much, do we.”

What are we going to say to Scarpelli when he asks? was on both their minds as they hopped in their car and drove off to turn in their report at the precinct house.

Later that same morning, Angie, barely asleep, heard her father's voice calling her name. Startled, she sat up and looked at her clock on the bedside table, almost 10:30 AM.

"Angie, are you just waking up?" asked Luigi from downstairs.

Stretching, yawning, feeling disoriented, Angie called back, "Yes, I guess I overslept," not letting on that she had been up most of the night reliving her sighting of the strange man on the street. She was beginning to believe he was the card-player killer everybody whispered about late last night.

"Angie, get dressed and come downstairs. Two detectives going door to door and talking to everyone on the block are here about what happened last night."

Dumbfounded and scared, Angie inhaled to quell her dizziness. She cleared her throat and answered, "Be down as soon as I can," as she felt the heat of her blood rush to her head and beads of perspiration form along her hairline across her forehead.

While dressing and brushing her teeth, Angie revisited her thoughts from the night before, trying to anticipate what questions these detectives might ask her. Descending the stairs, she thought, *Pull yourself together. You've seen many things, some good and some bad, and you can handle anything a couple of cops can throw at you.*

The first thing Angie saw upon stepping into the living room was Caterina, Luigi, JJ, and the two detectives seated around the dining table, drinking coffee. She walked over, sat at the table, a calm coming over her, and greeted the detectives after Luigi introduced her.

Detectives Daniel Scarpelli and David Gottlieb introduced themselves with a handshake.

Scarpelli opened, "Angie, we're going door to door, talking to everyone on this block and the next one. We want to find out if you saw anything regarding the shooting incident last night. We already asked your other family members here. Can you tell us where you were last night and at what time you got home?"

"I was hanging out with my friend, Diana, at her house until I left to come home around 11:00 PM."

"Where does your friend live?"

"On Metropolitan, a couple of blocks away."

"Did you see or hear anything on your walk home?" Gottlieb asked.

"Nothing unusual."

She mused *I did hear someone. And at the same time as the shooting. What am I going to do? I have to tell the truth. Oh no, I just lied!*

After further discussion alone with Caterina and Luigi, Scarpelli and Gottlieb thanked them, said goodbye, and left the house. Angie sighed and felt relieved, albeit also achingly disturbed about seeing that stranger last night and, of course, the lie that she just told.

The Carpellos went about their day after the detectives left. Standing in the kitchen, Caterina asked Angie, “What would you like to eat? You slept later than usual, and it’s almost lunchtime. You must be hungry. I will make you something.”

Angie didn’t respond.

“Don’t you feel well, honey?”

Angie hesitated to answer but then said, “I think I am coming down with a cold or something.”

“I’ll make you some soup, and after you eat, you go upstairs to your room and rest.”

“OK, mom, I will.”

She finished only half of her soup before she went upstairs. Laying on her bed, she felt the ruminations return, making her a little dizzy. This time, a cold sweat came over her.

What am I going to do? I lied to the police and in front of my mom and dad no less, which means I lied to them, too. I did see that man’s face. I need to tell the truth.”

She drifted to sleep again.

* * *

From somewhere he knew was safe, the mysterious Stevie "Snots" Matteo phoned his handler, Molinari, who had ordered the hit on Conselyea.

"The 'take-out was delivered, but we may have a slight problem. A girl may have seen me."

Molinari fumed, "What the fuck are you telling me? How could you be so sloppy? You're supposed to clean up messes, not make them! What the fuck happened?"

"She came out of nowhere. I headed up Conselyea after the delivery and saw her at the corner of Leonard. Who knows, maybe she didn't even see me."

'Molinari raged, "Well, did she or didn't she? What are you, some sort of moron? Did she or didn't she see you?"

Snots, alarmed now, was thinking. *In this business, I could wind up like the mark.*

"Mr. Molinari, I could tie up those loose ends if you want me to."

"Just do your fucking job! Lay low, for now, Snots. I'll be in touch. " *This guy's losing it, really fucked up! I've just about lost all my patience. First, he blabs about Wei being Chinese, almost screws up the hit on Fatso, and now this! I got no faith in the creep!* he thought.

Meanwhile, detectives Scarpelli and Gottlieb returned to their precinct house and compared notes with Bolleri and McCaffrey. They looked at each other on hearing the part where Scarpelli and Gottlieb had interviewed a teenage girl, Angie Carpello, listed as walking home from her friend's house on Metropolitan Avenue a little after 11:00 PM. This tidbit lined up with the information they received from Mr. Portinari and Mrs. Rossi about seeing a teenage girl pass by each of their houses around the same time.

Before Gottlieb finished his verbal report, Bolleri interjected, "Whoa, whoa, wait right there."

All eyes in the room were on him.

"Me and my partner here interviewed two people on Leonard who said they saw a teenage girl around that time and in that vicinity.

Looking at Scarpelli and Gottlieb, "You two may need to talk to this Angie Carpello again," said McCaffrey.

"When we talked to her, she said she saw nothing out of the ordinary and didn't seem alarmed or like she was hiding something," Gottlieb told the other guys.

Scarpelli made a mental note of the conflicting reports and dismissed for the time being any more discussion on the subject. He figured that at any moment, he would be getting a call from Molinari, who knew that he knew Snots' name was on the contract. What he didn't count on was the anger in Molinari's tone when he did call.

"Scarpelli, Snots fucked up! He just told me about a loose end, some girl who might have seen his delivery."

"Yeah, we're aware of a teenage girl. What are you going to do about Snots?"

"I'm not sure, but I told him to lay low for now!"

"Victor, I don't want to know the details."

"I wasn't gonna tell you anyways, Scarpelli, and maybe I shouldn't have told you that much. I'm just so pissed!"

"Gotcha. Let me know if you need me for anything. I have to go." With that, Scarpelli hung up on Molinari.

On the other end, Molinari thought about bringing Wei in on this but, for the moment, decided to forget his troubles. Instead, he poured himself a Cutty.

* * *

Caterina walked upstairs to check on Angie and see how she was feeling. She found her lying on the bed, staring at the ceiling.

"*Principessa*, what is the matter?"

Angie started crying.

"Oh, mommy, I saw something I should not have, and I'm very scared. I'm not sure if I should tell you because then you will know, too. I don't know what to do. I want to tell the truth, but I sort of lied to you and dad and the two detectives. I committed a mortal sin, and now I can't go to confession because the priest will know. I don't want anybody to get into trouble."

Angie rambled on, sobbing uncontrollably. Caterina put her arms around her daughter and calmed her.

"Sweet baby-girl, tell me what happened. You know your dad, and I will always protect you and Jenny."

After some minutes and once she felt reassured, Angie told her mom exactly what happened on the street. When finished, she let Caterina put two fingers to her lips, telling her, "What you told me stays in this house. I will tell your dad. You are not to mention this to anyone, not even Jenny. This information has to stay with the three of us only. Do you hear me?"

"But I committed a mortal sin, and if I don't go to confession, I will go to hell when I die!"

"Listen to me! You are not to mention this to anyone, not even a priest. You gave the police your answer. You're not going to hell when you die. Sometimes in life, there are bigger things at risk, and, in this case, you have no choice but to keep your mouth shut; otherwise, if you talk, you put me, your dad, and your sister Jenny in danger! Do you understand me?!"

Angie nodded, her head now buried deep into her mother's shoulder.

"Angie, there are some very bad people in this neighborhood, and, baby girl, they are very mean. They would not think twice about harming you. You may have lied to us, but you did the right thing telling me now, and you must say nothing more."

Angie pulled back, looked her mom straight in the eyes, smiled a little, and agreed. Each understood their pact.

Angie, soothed by Caterina's words, cried soft tears as her mom stood up to go out of the room.

"Stay here and rest, my dear. I'll bring you some dinner."

Caterina walked to the top of the stairwell and turned.

"Remember, no more talk of this. If you, or we, are approached by the police again, we will say not one single word of what you saw. You were coming home from your friend's house, and you walked straight down Metropolitan to Lorimer and then to Conselyea. That was the route you took. You said "Hello" to the Vegas sitting on their stoop as you walked on our block. So that is it, there's nothing more to say."

When Luigi returned home from having a beer at Chichi's with a friend, Caterina relayed Angie's story.

"Madonna Mia, why did this have to happen to my daughter, my sweet daughter?!"

At first, he was beside himself with mixed emotions and rage. Calmed a little, whirling, he spoke to his wife again.

"Caterina, did you tell Angie that she must not repeat this story to anyone, including Jenny?"

"Yes, I did, and I'm sure she will not say a word to anyone. Oh, Luigi, our Angie was so worried that she had committed a mortal sin. She wanted to go to confession."

Luigi retorted, "She did the right thing today when she lied to those detectives in front of us."

They hugged and agreed.

"Angie could hardly eat. She had some soup and went up to bed."

"Then I'll talk to her in the morning."

In the morning, Luigi checked in on his distressed daughter. After he knocked on her bedroom door, she let him into her room and sat on the edge of her bed.

"Angie, dear, your mother told me what happened."

"I'm so sorry, Dad. I know I told a lie, a sin."

"Listen to me..." He paused to let his rising blood pressure subside.

"Dad, I lied to the detectives because I did see something happen..."

Luigi cut her off there, “Angie, you heard nothing. You were walking by and, not knowing what you think you saw, you saw nothing.”

“But lying is a sin, Dad!”

“Angie, just because you think you heard something doesn’t mean you have to tell anyone you did. Besides, you have to think about what’s best for the whole family here.”

Angie understood Luigi’s message and resolved to keep quiet.

“Dad, I get the point. I won’t tell a soul!”

* * *

The four detectives involved with the investigation walked out of the conference room. They had just agreed that Scarpelli and Gottlieb, using information they got from Bolleri and McCaffrey, would go back to the Carpello house and interview Angie and her parents again.

“Daniel, it looks like that girl had to see something, don’t ya think? Do ya think, if she saw anything, that she told her parents?” asked Gottlieb of his partner.

"I'm not sure that even if she saw something, she would tell us. You know how that neighborhood is; WB people got that no-speak thing going on. They see things, but they don't talk."

"I hear ya. 'Look and see what you see, which is nothing.'"

"Yeah, like a tacit consent; I heard about it. I doubt we'll get anything out of that girl, especially if she already confided to her parents."

"Exactly, they're never gonna tell us."

"So, we'll go see them anyway."

* * *

On the Sunday morning following the shooting, Angie woke up to the aroma of fresh meatballs frying on the stove downstairs. Rested, she felt stronger since she confided to her parents. As she descended the stairs, the food aromas enveloped her, bringing her appetite back.

Walking into the living room and seeing her dad seated at the dining-room table, reading the Sunday paper, she said, "Good morning, Daddy."

Luigi put his paper down on the table, stood, walked over to his oldest daughter, and put his arms around her.

"Angie, I love you very much. We all agree that the whole story remains in this house, never to be repeated. This is the only way your mom and I can protect you."

"I know, daddy. I was so afraid that I committed a mortal sin, but now I understand what's at stake. I will never say a word to anyone, I swear. I love you, dad!"

They hugged again, watched by Caterina, who approved. JJ was upstairs in her room, presumably reading another book.

Later in the afternoon, when the street lamps shined across Conselyea, the front-door bell rang. Detectives Scarpelli and Gottlieb—they had known not to come earlier and interfere in the Sunday afternoon dinner—were calling on the Carpello family again.

Seeing them through the front window, Luigi whispered to his daughter, "Remember, not a word."

He opened the door and bid the men, "Gentlemen, come inside."

Caterina offered espresso and put out a choice selection of Italian pastries in front of them on the table.

This time, Gottlieb started the questioning and directed it toward Angie.

"So, on Friday night, you told us that you left your friend's house around 11:00 PM and that, as you were walking home, you didn't see or hear anything. Is that right?"

"Yes, that's right," replied Angie.

"And what blocks did you walk on to get home?"

"I walked down Metropolitan Avenue to Lorimer Street, made a right turn, and then walked down Conselyea Street toward my house."

"Well," Scarpelli interjected, "We heard from a few people who live on Leonard Street that they saw a girl pass by around 11:00 PM, but you say you didn't walk home by way of Leonard Street, is that correct?"

"Yes, that's right."

Luigi looked at the detectives, saying, "If that is the way my daughter says she walked home, then that is the way. My daughter is a truthful girl, and, as I recall, she also told both of you yesterday that she did not hear or see anything. She couldn't because she didn't walk on Leonard Street on Friday night..."

Everyone at the table went silent. Sipping espresso and tasting the pastries, the detectives listened as Luigi spoke again, "I'm not sure what the people you spoke to told you they saw, but it wasn't my Angie."

With that, Scarpelli and Gottlieb knew they were done. They stood up, thanked the Carpello family, and left the house. Crossing the street to their unmarked car, Scarpelli said, "Maybe it wasn't this Angie girl that people saw on Leonard."

"I don't think so," countered Gottlieb.

“Well, if she walked down Metropolitan to Lorimer, she would have passed Leonard Street, not walked on it.”

“I think you’re right about that.”

The next day at the precinct, Bolleri, McCaffrey, Scarpelli, and Gottlieb hashed out the second interview with Angie, trying to reconcile what she said with what the people living on Leonard Street had seen and told them.

McCaffrey opined, “I think Angie was the girl on Leonard Street.”

The three other detectives looked at him, and Scarpelli asked, “John, why do you think that?”

“I’m not sure yet.”

CHAPTER 23: THE NOOSE TIGHTENS

Intending to brief Molinari about the investigation into the shooting, Detective Scarpelli entered the Felsina Social Club through the back door in the alley between Mott and Mulberry Streets.

Sitting in the back room far away from prying eyes and drinking Cutty with his handler, Scarpelli debriefed about the ongoing police investigation and related activities.

"McCaffrey suspects that a teenage girl from the neighborhood, who was walking on Metropolitan Avenue, may have seen the shooting go down. He also thinks she may have been the same girl walking on Leonard Street that night."

"What makes him think that? It doesn't make sense. The same girl walking on two different streets?" asked Molinari.

"He says he's got a gut feeling on this. I don't know what he is getting at. Gottlieb and I interviewed the Carpellos twice—the Angie girl's parents—and the Angie girl, too. Each time, when questioned, she told us that on that night, she walked on Metropolitan to Lorimer Street, and then on Conselyea to her house."

Molinari sipped his drink, looked into Scarpelli's eyes, and said, "So, two people say they saw a girl on Leonard Street, one walking in one direction and another walking in the other direction. And this was at the same time this Angie says she was on Metropolitan?"

"Yessir, Mr. Molinari."

"Snots says that he thinks a girl saw him after he made the hit, and this girl was walking on Leonard Street while he ran up Conselyea toward Graham. Maybe McCaffrey's right. It's a loose end. I'll look into it. You just keep doing what you're doing. Good report. Scarpelli."

With that, another thick wad of cash inside an envelope passed across the table, and Scarpelli went away.

Later the same afternoon, Wei entered the Felsina Social Club through the same back alley. He had been summoned for a meeting with Molinari, who would bring him up to speed on the WB police investigation and the fresh intel he received from Scarpelli.

Wei demurred the offered Cutty, reminding his boss that it wasn't his style to drink. Molinari, of course, knew this, but he still liked to tease his favorite cleaner, taking perverse pleasure in watching his pride flinch at the offerings, considering how invincible he was out in the field.

Today wouldn't be the last flinch Wei would feel inside, even if he never showed it on the outside, because his employer brought up Angie Carpello as a "P.I." (Person of Interest). Stunned to hear her name, he played it cool. Glued to his chair across from Molinari, Wei listened with acute attention and a stoic attitude.

"We might be in trouble here. We know this Angie girl has told the police nothing, but they're sure to keep snooping around. I have a man on the inside, keeping his ear to the ground on that. One of his men thinks she's the one who can identify my shooter, and we can't have that. You know what I mean?"

Wei responded evenly, "Let me handle girl. Angie from WB. We met. Neighborhood keep to self what see and hear. She trust me. I contact, bring you good news."

"Yeah, I heard about that say-nothing agreement they got there. I kinda like it."

Hesitant, but thinking what an asset Wei had already been to him, and about his *paesano* Abatelli back in Nola, Molinari greenlighted Wei's request.

"I handle her, no problem."

"I'm sure you will, Wei. I'm counting on it."

After Wei left the social club, Molinari called Gap to update him.

"All we know, Joey, is that the two locals who saw the girl in front of their houses can't describe her, and neither can Snots. Scarpelli told me only one Detective, McCaffrey, thinks it was Angie who witnessed the hit."

"Well, it's almost two weeks out, and the girl's been interviewed twice by the cops and stuck to the same story. If that holds, we can let it go. I'm not too concerned about this McCaffrey guy's gut, for now. So far, no one has fingered her with any hard evidence."

Molinari, lying, embellished his reply, "*I asked* Wei to speak to Angie directly. He's familiar with her. He said he would handle her if she is the one. I'll keep you posted, Joey."

"*Grazie*."

CHAPTER 24: AT LAST, CONNECTION!

Wei kept to back alleys as he made his way home. He felt sad and desperate because he had developed a need to protect Angie. Thinking about the 'tacit' thing that hung over WB, he hoped that she would stick to her story.

If she's the girl walking on Leonard Street, the one who saw Snots that night—Wei by now had figured out Snots' "M.O.," and the signs were all over that hit—*she's in trouble!*

To keep her alive and to make sure she would keep her mouth shut, he knew that somehow he had to get to Angie before McCaffery or Snots did. He also knew the time finally had come to meet her in person one on one, even though it might not be quite the way he would have planned it.

The following Friday evening, Angie walked home alone after hanging out with friends at McCarren Park. Suddenly, Wei pulled her into a narrow space between a couple of row houses. She started to scream, but he put his hand over her mouth. Coming out of the shadows as she struggled, Wei looked into Angie's eyes and, seeing her fear, revealed himself to her.

Astonished, Angie recognized him but didn't know what to think or feel.

Her thoughts raced, *I know this man, and I don't know him. I'm scared but somehow relieved. What does he want?*

"I take you place to talk. I protect you."

"From what? I can't go anywhere with you. My parents will expect me at home."

She struggled to get free.

"Calm down. I protect you."

"I can't go with you. I'm afraid."

"This very important, Angie. You and family in danger."

"You know my name?"

"Yes. My job to know this."

"Are you a cop?"

"No, I remember you. I remember you shout at me and..."

She cut him off, "You deserved that!"

"I tip my hat. I know you saw."

"You only touched it."

"My signal. I like you, Angie, and I not harm you now."

Angie tried again to free herself, but her emotions took over; she sobbed and had trouble catching her breath.

Wei saw that she was having a panic attack and wanted to console her, but he decided he needed to be firm instead.

"Angie, do as I say! You and family not get hurt. Call parents. Tell them you stay with friend tonight. Just do it!"

Startled to hear the demanding tone of his words, she looked him in the eyes and consented, "I will do what you say."

She made the call from a nearby street-corner phone booth. After reassuring her parents that she would be snuggly tucked into bed at her best friend Valentina's house for the night, she hung up the phone and got in the car with Wei.

Wei drove to his apartment in Chinatown. On arrival, he and Angie entered the building and sat at a table centered in his gym's dark and nearly empty space.

Switching a light on, he said, "Angie, no fear. No one important know we here now. This my plan to protect you and your family."

She looked at Wei and surmised this had to do with the shooting she had heard and the man she saw running away. She steeled herself for the question she knew was coming.

"Angie, people talk you girl who saw shooting."

Angie's thoughts scattered! *"Do I trust this man? Is he trying to set me up? Is he really here to protect me? Should I tell him the truth? My parents said the story needs to stay within the walls of our home. I don't know what to do."*

"What shooting?"

Her act did not dissuade him.

"Angie, please, be straight with me. I feel bond first time we meet years ago on stoop."

"I remember," she said quietly.

"You sassy that day. Tell what stoop is!"

She returned his provocative remark with a carefree smile.

Wei continued.

"True, you right. I think of you. One day, Nola, I think I see you. You there?"

Angie looked at Wei quizzically, "No, I wasn't there, but last year, I thought I caught a glimpse of you behind the Chinese food stand at the Shrine of the Madonna Feast. That was you, wasn't it?"

"Yes, I help Chinese family."

Angie, relaxing, thought *I knew it!*

A smug smile crossed her face, which Wei either missed or ignored.

"Let me get to point! You come home from friend, hear gunshot, see man. Two people on Leonard see girl, maybe you, walk past houses. One see girl walk to Conselyea, other see walk Metropolitan Avenue. Angie, you that girl, right?"

Angie stared at Wei and tried to comprehend. *Who is this man who says he wants to protect me? What are his real plans for me?*

Her mind flashbacked. She remembered that she had retraced her steps to get away from what she heard and from the stranger. Panic streaked through her again as she also realized that two people saw her walking on Leonard.

"Is what you're telling me true? Two people saw a girl walking on Leonard Street? Did the police speak to her? How did you hear about this?" she asked.

"Angie, I tell truth. I have sources. I not risk meet if not think police or someone order hit can find girl was you."

Inhaling deeply, she decided to give it all up.

"That night around eleven, I was walking home from a friend's house on Metropolitan Avenue. I got to Leonard Street and made a right turn to walk home on Conselyea. As I just about got to the corner, I heard two clicking sounds and turned."

She looked to see if Wei was listening, and, seeing that he was, she continued.

"I saw a man walk toward Graham Avenue. Right away, I realized I was in the wrong place at the wrong time. So, I back-tracked my steps on Leonard Street toward Metropolitan and, when I got to Lorimer Street, I made a right turn toward my block."

"That all?"

"Yes, everything. At first, I didn't know what those clicking sounds were, but after I heard the card player was shot and killed, I realized that was probably a silencer."

"You see man?" Wei asked.

"Yes."

"If you see gunman, and police never stop, question you, wear you down to tell truth, that put you in harm's way! You tell parents?"

Angie started to shake and cry. She could not speak, so he spoke for her.

"Okay, you tell them. I know parents not tell."

Wei had Angie's attention, and he continued.

"... Angie, listen me! You walk down Metropolitan to Lorimer and house on Conselyea. You more than block away; you not hear or see anything, OK? That your story..."

She nodded.

"... People on Leonard not describe you. Hitman cannot..."

She nodded again, more at ease.

"... You not tell parents we meet... less they know, better for you and family."

He walked to a closet and retrieved some items that he handed to her.

"You through a lot. Take blanket, pillow, sleep on couch. You safe here. I get you back tomorrow."

The next morning, Wei woke Angie and served her hot green tea. Sitting at the table with her, he told her, "You safe from now on. No worry, okay?"

"Okay," she replied, resigned to whatever would come, knowing Wei was in charge and that there was no need for more talk based on the circumstances.

Wei then discussed a long-term plan that he wanted them to execute together, designed to keep her free from harm and danger, if possible.

"Angie, when meet again, we not bring attention to you and me. You see me, I see you, here, there. We act cool."

"Understood."

"And this meet not take place."

Angie looked around, wondering what to do next or where to go, and Wei picked up her thought.

"Car pick us up. We go Williamsburg Bridge, exit Marcy Avenue at Broadway, drop you, you walk home."

When they got there, Angie asked, "Where will you go?"

"No worry about me. I fine! And you, too; I have your back. Trust me."

Angie kissed Wei's cheek, got out, and walked home.

The car's driver transported Wei to Bushwick, Brooklyn. He left the vehicle on Myrtle Avenue and waited. In less than a minute, a black Cadillac pulled up to the curb in front of him. He got in the back seat.

Gap asked, "How did it go?"

"I vouch for her. She not girl on Leonard," Wei lied.

"Great job, Wei. I'm relieved to hear this because my family and the Ambrezias, specifically Angie's grandfather Giuseppe, go back to Italy."

Gap noticed the lipstick on Wei's cheek, "What's that all about?"

"That? That gratitude," he answered, rubbing the lipstick off.

Gap smiled and shook Wei's hand, "Where can I drop you, *Peter*?" It was the first time he addressed Wei by his first name.

"Wherever convenient."

"No... Let me drop you off where you're headed; that's the least I can do for you."

"Chinatown."

Wei exited Gap's car at the corner of Kenmare and Mott Streets and tipped his hat to Gap.

Gap leaned to the open window and said, "Take care, ***paesano***!"

Smiling broadly, Peter Wei walked like he owned Chinatown's streets. Sure that the Gallucci Family welcomed him as more than just a good cleaner, he felt his future was bright.

More comforting was that he knew that he had altered the course of Angie's life and, by protecting her, had reconciled with honor the death of his parents!

ABOUT CAROLYN ANGIOLILLO

Carolyn Angiolillo was born and raised in Williamsburg Brooklyn, New York.

A graduate of St. John's University in Queens, New York, she earned a Bachelor of Arts degree in Environmental Studies and a Master of Arts degree in Government & Politics.

Carolyn lives in Longboat Key, Florida.

A Brooklyn Saga Stories from the Stoop is her first published novel.

cangiolillo@gmail.com

ABOUT RONALD JOSEPH KULE

Acclaimed author, biographer, novelist, and ghostwriter Ronald Joseph Kule hails from Bogota, Colombia. His Polish-American father and Colombian-Chilean mother paint-brushed his life-canvas with wanderlust. Consequently, he came to appreciate many ethnic differences and similarities by spending time in more than 39 countries.

Kule smiles and laughs easily but prefers to inspire happiness through his books.

"If you curl up with one of my books and find yourself breathless, provoked, inspired, changed, and feeling like you undertook an important, emotionally satisfying journey, I will have done my job as your author." – Ron Kule

---

Living in Clearwater, Florida, Kule writes across several genres. For clients, his specialties are biography and historical fiction. His published titles consistently earn five stars on review.

BOOKS BY RONALD JOSEPH KULE

CAROLINA BASEBALL PRESSURE MAKES DIAMONDS, leatherbound & eBook, *Pressure Makes Diamonds a Timeless Tale of America's Greatest Pastime* (J. David Miller & Ron Kule)

POETIC JUSTICE ~ *CAROLINA BASEBALL 2012 ~ The Historic Run for the Three-peat* (softcover, KuleBooks LLC).

CHEF TELL The Biography Of America's Pioneer TV Showman Chef, forewords by Regis Philbin & Chef Walter Staib. (Hardcover, Kindle, Audiobook, Skyhorse Publishing)

LISTEN MORE SELL MORE VOLUME ONE ~ The Anatomy of a Sale; Swedish edition: *LYSSNA MER SAL MER*; Spanish edition: *ESCUCHA MAS VENDE MAS*; Russian edition (coming 2021): *БОЛЬШЕ СЛУШАЕШЬ БОЛЬШЕ ПРОДАШЬ КНИГА ПЕРВАЯ: АНАТОМИЯ ПРОДАЖИ.* (KuleBooks LLC) (softcover, KuleBooks LLC)

RUINED BY MURDER ADDICTED TO LOVE (mystery/romance, softcover & eBook novel, KuleBooks LLC)

THUNDERCLOUD (The Oddities of a Young Man's Journey to Manhood) (magical realism, softcover & eBook novel, KuleBooks LLC)

HAUNTED ROBOTS (James Patrick Warner & Ronald Joseph Kule, story by Michael E. Noll) (sci-fi softcover & eBook, The Haunted Robot LLC)

LIVING BEYOND IMPOSSIBLE ~ The Terry Hitchcock Story, foreword by Tracy Repchuk (Biography, softcover & eBook, KuleBooks LLC)

LISTEN MORE SELL MORE VOLUME TWO: The Mechanics of Selling. (softcover, KuleBooks LLC)

MINNIE BOLTON'S OLDE VERMONTER RECIPES (with Terry Hitchcock) (Softcover & eBook, KuleBooks LLC)

CONVERSATIONS WITH ANIMALS (Farm Girl to Veterinarian ~ Dr. Ava Frick Story), with Dr. Ava Frick, DVM, February 9, 2021 release date) (Biography, hardcover, softcover & eBook, KuleBooks LLC).

The 3rd and final series volume, *LISTEN MORE SELL MORE VOLUME THREE: How to Handle Objections by Tone,* (softcover, KuleBooks LLC [Fall 2021])

To purchase books or commission the author's services, contact:

HTTPS://RONKULEBOOKS.COM

Printed in the USA
CPSIA information can be obtained
at www.ICGtesting.com
LVHW020728091223
766038LV00017B/1127